OFFBEAT

Megan Clendenan

ORCA BOOK PUBLISHERS

Library and Archives Canada Cataloguing in Publication

Clendenan, Megan, 1977–, author
Offbeat / Megan Clendenan.
(Orca limelights)

Issued in print and electronic formats.
ISBN 978-1-4598-1792-0 (softcover).—ISBN 978-1-4598-1793-7 (PDF).—
ISBN 978-1-4598-1794-4 (EPUB)

I. Title. II. Series: Orca limelights
PS8605.L5413O34 2018   jc813'.6   C2017-907951-4
C2017-907952-2

First published in the United States, 2018
Library of Congress Control Number: 2018933712

Summary: In this high-interest novel for teen readers, Rose loves
the fiddle and is determined to become a folk sensation. But her
mom is insisting she study only classical violin.

*Orca Book Publishers is dedicated to preserving the environment and
has printed this book on Forest Stewardship Council® certified paper.*

Orca Book Publishers gratefully acknowledges the support for
its publishing programs provided by the following agencies:
the Government of Canada through the Canada Book Fund and the
Canada Council for the Arts, and the Province of British Columbia
through the BC Arts Council and the Book Publishing Tax Credit.

Edited by Tanya Trafford
Cover design by Rachel Page
Cover photography by Christopher Kimmel/Getty Images

ORCA BOOK PUBLISHERS
orcabook.com

Printed and bound in Canada.

21 20 19 18 • 4 3 2 1

For Geri

One

M y fingers fly. They buzz and dart like a swarm of bees on the neck of my fiddle. I tap my toe to keep the beat, but I feel like jumping. Our group is rehearsing for the last time before the Blackberry Music Festival on the Olympic Peninsula, one of the biggest deals for folk music in the whole region. The tension is as tight as our strings.

"Okay, let's take a break," says Ms. O'Krancy, our music teacher, who looks like a wispy-haired elf queen. She puts her fiddle down and goes to check her notes.

"Rose." I feel a sharp nudge in my left shoulder. Shilo is poking me with her bow. We have been best friends since second grade. "Want to come over after school?"

1

"I'm there," I say. Anything not to go home.

I turn back as Ms. O'Krancy claps for our attention at the front. "Ladies and gentlemen! As you well know, we leave tomorrow." She makes a point of looking at each one of us. Our group has ten members, and we are all here today. "You've all practiced hard for the past two years for this chance to perform on the main stage at the festival. You'll be in front of the biggest audience you've had yet. But please remember, this festival is not only about performance. It's also about participation. You can learn so much from the other musicians. You've got five days to attend workshops of your choice—they've got everything from Irish to jazz to..." Her voice fades as I picture myself standing onstage, playing to a massive, moving crowd. "...and on the last day of the festival the Grand Prize winner of the fiddle contest will get onstage with Lunar."

Wait, what? The group is buzzing. Like most of them, I can't go a day without listening to Lunar, a band known for its blend of Celtic, Cajun and Latin music. There's no other band like it touring right now. If I could go onstage with Lunar, the world could just stop. I need to find out more.

"Okay, on to the Irish jig. Let's push the pace to double time!" Ms. O'Krancy says.

We raise our fiddles and wait for our cue.

"Don't worry. My mom never talks to your mom because she never sees her," Shilo whispers. I'm supposed to go home after school and practice for my classical violin lessons. My mom thinks they're my ticket to the youth symphony.

"One and two and three and..." Ms. O'Krancy counts us in, and we play, in close to perfect unison. The music erases the chatter in my head. For this moment, I'm good.

* * *

After school I see Shilo standing by her mom's old-style orange VW bug.

"Hi, Anna. Thanks for picking us up," I say, wearing my parent-winning smile. I shove my fiddle case in the backseat, between the empty stainless-steel water bottles and piles of cloth shopping bags, and hoist myself onto the cleanest side. Their car smells like dog because of their springer spaniel, Jeffrey. I don't mention it.

"Shilo and I were just talking about the music festival. Looks like you two will get to share a room with me," Anna says as she hops into the driver's seat. "I guess your mom won't be joining us because of her work schedule?" I don't need to answer because Anna is now focused on moving the car through the lineup of other parents. I let Anna grill Shilo about her school day while I stare out the window, playing tunes in my head.

"Hey, so how about that contest?" Shilo asks from the front seat.

"I need to find out more," I say. "Let's check out their website when we get to your place." We pull up to Shilo's house minutes later and walk through the wild jungle of plants in the front yard. Anna heads straight to the kitchen. I know she's probably making us a snack. Some home-made banana bread or maybe those weird but tasty seaweed chips. Shilo opens her laptop and types *Blackberry Festival* into the search engine.

"Check out the main page," she says. There's a huge picture of a guy onstage with a guitar, his long hair pulled back in a ponytail. He and a fiddler are holding hands as though they are about to bow. She's wearing a sparkly shirt and tons of beaded jewelry. "This is going to be so fun!"

"Click on that button there," I say, wishing I was the girl on the home page.

Blackberry Fiddle Contest
- *Come on out and show off your best tunes.*
- *First round: Day 1 at the Garden Stage.*
- *Each contestant will play one tune of choice.*
- *The Top 20 will advance to the final round on Day 6.*
- *Maybe you will be the lucky Grand Prize winner who gets to perform onstage with Lunar!*

"OMG, can you imagine how awesome that would be?" I say. I click on another link.

The People's Choice Award
- *Back by popular demand!*
- *VOTE for YOUR favorite performer from the first round on Day 1.*
- *Winner gets their own 15-minute slot at the Marketplace on Day 3.*

"Wait," says Shilo. "Does that mean that some lucky someone gets to perform their own little mini concert?"

"I think so," I say. "So we need to practice! I'm going to sign up tonight." I need to win that spot. Shilo has a solo in our performance because she also plays the Irish flute. I really wish I had a solo too. I want to push myself, to see what I can do. I want to be heard. We play until just before dinnertime and then Anna offers to give me a ride home.

"Do you have your key?" Anna asks. I can tell by her voice that she's not exactly comfortable dropping me off at an empty house.

"I do, thanks," I say with my parent-winning smile back on. I don't want her to feel bad about not inviting me for dinner. She knows my mom works late. "And thanks so much for driving me. You rock." I hop out and wave, my grin still plastered on, key in hand. I walk up the three steps to our townhouse and don't look back.

Two

"Good morning," my mom says as I enter the kitchen. She looks over her laptop and stops typing as my toast pops up. She noticed me. She even made me toast. I'm surprised. Sometimes I'm halfway through eating before she looks up, usually with a confused face like, *When did Rose walk in?*

"Hi, Mom," I say, crashing down into the padded kitchen chair. "Hey, can you pass me—"

"Just give me a second to finish this email," she interrupts and is once again lost in electronics. She is dressed in her usual navy suit, her hair perfectly straightened. She just made partner in her law firm. Apparently law-firm partners need to keep three times as many stacks of paper on their kitchen tables. There's barely room for my plate and glass of orange juice. I reach over and grab the peanut butter.

"What were you going to ask?" she murmurs as she types away on her laptop.

"Never mind," I say. "I got it myself."

"Okay, I've got about five minutes before my next conference call starts, and I've got all my material prepped. So I'd like to give you your birthday present now." I munch my toast and don't bother answering. I don't want to waste my five minutes of scheduled time with questions.

"As you know, your father had a beautiful violin. What you don't know is that in his will he asked that it be gifted to you when you turned fourteen." My mom is using her lawyer tone, serious and flat. I grip my toast, suspended halfway to my mouth. We sit silently, the only sound the chickadees singing outside our window.

"Mom, that's amazing," I finally sputter. My dad died two years ago. He was the one who always got me the perfect gift. Most of the gifts I can remember my mom giving me seemed like they were bought for another person. Like the leather jacket with the frills on the bottom that I got for my thirteenth birthday. I hate frills. Or, for my twelfth birthday, the party at a pottery studio even though I don't give a crap about art. I turned fourteen last week and wasn't at all surprised when she wished me a quick "Happy birthday" on her way out the door and said she would give me my present later. I just assumed that meant she hadn't bought it yet. "Where is it?"

"I've put it in the den. It's yours now to take to the festival." I can see her grinding her teeth. "But..."

Here we go. There's always a but.

My mom hesitates. "I know you're going to this music festival. And I hope you have a good time. But the Celtic group isn't the youth symphony. And the symphony is where you need to be to prepare for getting a classical music degree at university."

We've had this conversation about a jillion times. If I tried to figure out how many more times we'll have this fight before I actually go to university, I think my brain would overheat.

"You would learn all the classical symphonies—Bach, Mozart, Beethoven. You might even make some new friends." As my mom gathers steam, her eyes look like they're about to pop out of her head. I imagine them taking flight from her sockets, springing out like they're jet-propelled. I have to choke back a laugh as I imagine searching for my mom's eyeballs in the kitchen sink.

"I've already told you that I want to play Celtic music and maybe go live in Ireland someday," I say, wishing her meeting would start.

"I just want you to be practical." She checks her phone again. "Here's the thing. I can't continue to pay for your violin lessons if you refuse to consider the youth symphony." She throws her shoulders back and stares me down.

"What? You won't pay for my lessons anymore? But they're classical!" Spit flies out as I speak.

"That may be, but you're only using them to improve your technique so you can play those fast songs. I understand music."

"Tunes, Mom. They're called tunes, not songs," I interrupt.

"You're going to have to show me you are truly serious about this instrument. Music lessons are expensive. Especially yours. I would pay for group lessons, but not private. Group lessons are much less expensive." I know my lessons cost quite a bit. But my teacher, who plays in the city orchestra, also loves Celtic music. When she sees I'm getting bored playing my classical pieces, she teaches me fiddle tunes to give me a break. We don't mention that to my mom.

"What?" I feel my hands start to shake. "I play all the time. I don't waste time watching TV. What more do you want from me?"

"Show me you're serious about your musical future. Then you get to keep your private lessons."

"This is not fair," I say. I think of all the scales and arpeggios I do every night after dinner. The pain in my fingertips after practicing for two hours.

"Sorry, I have to join the conference call," my mom says. That's my cue to leave. I walk down the hall to the den. This was my dad's room. On the desk is a black fiddle case. I walk over and zip it open. I touch the black silk that covers the fiddle and slip it off. And there it is. Beautiful red-brown wood. The color always reminds me of a fire about to burst out. I can't stop the salty tears. Every happy memory I have from before he died includes my dad playing this fiddle.

My favorite times were when he played with his friends. They would sit in a circle in our cozy kitchen. Dan, the guitar player, would be grooving with his whole body. Nellie, the other fiddler, would have this giant smile, while Bruce rocked an Irish flute like you've never seen a big guy rocking a flute. My mom would even grab spoons and keep a beat going while they played. She would laugh as they picked up the tempo until it was so fast that only my dad was left playing. He would end with a flourish and look around with his big grin. "Too slow for you all to bother?"

I place the fiddle on my shoulder. It feels like mine and his at the same time. I put it down to take out the bow and open the little compartment where my dad kept the rosin for the bow. It's empty. I feel around inside the case, trying to find the small round lump. My pinkie finger snags on a rip in the silk lining. I feel a rough edge of paper. I try to pull it out, but it's too far in.

I can hear my mom is still on the phone. She'll be a while. I grab the old-fashioned letter opener from the desk and use it to make a bigger tear in the lining. Now I can pull out the paper. It's a black-and-white photo of my mom and dad. He's playing his fiddle, and my mom is playing a flute. They're young. My mom almost looks like me. And I didn't even know she played the flute. I sit frozen, wondering why she never told me she played. And why she is so against me playing the music I like.

Three

've never been on an airplane before. The air tastes stale, used. I turn to Shilo, who is sitting next to me, reading the boring magazine from the seat pocket.

"Why haven't we left yet?" I say, crossing and uncrossing my legs. "I can't stand sitting here. I swear we were supposed to leave a half hour ago." I want to get there in time to rehearse before the first round.

In the seat behind me, one of the other girls, Emilia, asks a never-ending series of questions. "Ms. O'Krancy, will we have practice space? And will there be vegetarian food?" I see Shilo eyeing Murray, one of the two boys in our group. He has his mandolin out and is quietly strumming, his dark hair falling over one eye.

"I'm just glad I don't have to sit next to my mom," Shilo says, taking out a small mirror and checking out the latest orange streak in her hair. I like that my hair color almost matches the wood on my dad's—*my*—fiddle.

"Your mom's not so bad," I say.

"That's because she's not your mom," Shilo says. "Plus she likes you and doesn't make you eat seaweed. Though I kind of like the seaweed. It's salty."

"Yeah, well, at least she lets you choose your music," I say. "My mom told me when she gave me my dad's fiddle that I have to show her I'm serious about music or else she'll cancel my private lessons."

"What?" Shilo yelps. "That's completely insane. What are you going to do?"

"I have to win the fiddle contest," I say. "That should prove something. Even to her."

I check again to see if my mom has sent me a text. Nothing. Once we get to the festival, we're not allowed to use cell phones.

"Good morning, folks," the pilot's voice booms out on a scratchy loudspeaker. After he introduces himself, he gives us an update. Fog has delayed takeoff. "We hope to be in the air in approximately forty-five minutes. Thank you for your patience."

"Ughh! I am not patient," I say.

"What about the contest?" Shilo asks, turning to get Ms. O'Krancy's attention. "Could we actually miss the first round?"

"Oh, man," I say, slumping down in my seat. "I sure hope not."

* * *

Our plane finally lands in Seattle and we transfer to a minibus that will take us to the festival site. As we leave the city behind, it feels like the bus is moving so slowly we might as well be going backward. All I can think about is what will happen if I miss the fiddle contest. I imagine my mom calling Karen, my violin teacher, and canceling my lessons. Forever. Then signing me up for stupid group lessons. I'd be stuck with the kids who only want to try music for fun. I look out my window and see fields with rows and rows of vegetables.

"People live here," Shilo says, leaning over to see out the window. "See those little houses over there?

Apparently they all face the moon and are shaped like tiny pyramids. And people only eat food that they grow here, and they do yoga all the time."

"I can't believe they scheduled the first round for this afternoon," I say. "Why not tomorrow morning? What if we miss it?" We bump along the road into thick forest, where the fir and cedar trees completely shade out the sun. I spot several VW vans parked in the trees and a few tents set up off the road. The forest opens up again to a clearing.

"Look," I say, pointing. The clearing is completely jammed with tents, like a tiny village. "I bet that's where the spectators stay," I add. "Performers must stay somewhere else." I hope so anyway. It looks crowded to me. I can tell from the shocked look on Shilo's face that she thinks the same.

"Yeah, I don't think my mom would ever agree to stay in one of those tents," Shilo says. The bus keeps moving, and the forest closes in on us again. Then there's another clearing, this one with a giant pyramid-shaped building made of tea-colored cedar in the center. The building is surrounded by dozens of tents, but not the kind you sleep in. They're more like the kind you see at fairs, with tables under the canvas. A row of rainbow-colored awnings forms a path from the parking area to the tents.

"All right, everyone, listen up." Ms. O'Krancy stands. "We made it! Now we need to check in and get our performer badges. Don't lose them. Please remember you may circulate through the festival during the day and after dinner, but your curfew is nine o'clock. If you've signed up for the fiddle contest, grab your instrument and we'll head over as soon as you have your badge. It starts soon, but if you hurry you should still have a chance to compete."

"Look at that guy!" Shilo whispers loudly and points. I push her arm down and try to look casually where she pointed. A guy with long dark hair is weaving through the crowd. He's carrying a battered fiddle case on his back. He's wearing one of those slouchy knit caps even though it's summer. He walks like he knows exactly where he's going.

Outside the bus the dry June heat seeps into my skin. Shilo and I stick close to each other in the crowd. Everyone seems to be hugging each other. There are instrument cases everywhere, piled high on the ground with backpacks and taped-together suitcases. Tents stretch out in all directions, with all sorts of food on offer— donairs, fish tacos and fruit smoothies. A whole tent is devoted to mandolins. One of the tents has a giant silver coffee urn and a big sign that says *Bring your own mug. Pay what you can.*

"That's where we go." Ms. O'Krancy points toward a tent where there is a long line of people with papers in hand. I spot a group of kids sitting in a drum circle off to one side. I grab Shilo's hand and try not to look like a total staring idiot.

"Can you believe we're here?" she asks.

"We are totally ready to be here," I say. "But this lineup is going to drive me crazy."

"There he is again." Shilo nudges me and gestures with her head. It's the cute guy with the cap. "Are you going to try to talk to him?"

We watch him stroll up to the front of the line and give a high five to a young girl with a tiny fiddle case. She looks up at him like he's a rock star. He smiles and says something that makes her laugh.

"What is he doing?" I say as the girl lets him in line. I should have thought of doing that.

After what feels like hours, Shilo and I finally reach the front of the registration line. The guy in the cap has disappeared.

"Welcome!" A man and woman sit at a table stacked with a jumble of colored paper.

"Okay, you two are official performers, so here are your backstage passes," says the man. He hands us each a big laminated badge on a string. I take a quick peek. There's my name: Rose Callaghan.

"Do we still have time to make it to the fiddle contest?" I ask. My words tumble out so fast I sound like a crazed cartoon character.

"Well, it's already started, but I'm not really sure how far along they are," says the woman. "It's being held at the Garden Stage. To get there you follow the path behind us." She stands up in what feels like slow motion, turns around and points toward a forest trail. "Now here's your map, your meal tickets and your yurt assignment. Oh, and some cookie vouchers! Don't lose those. Any other questions?"

I couldn't care less about cookies right now. I grab the pile of paper from her hand.

"Thank you so much. No questions." I smile sweetly, and Shilo and I bolt toward the trail.

Four

I feel like I do just before I walk onstage to perform. Only right now I'm not sure where the stage is or whether I'll be too late. I check the map.

"Okay, here." I point. "We walk down this trail, like the woman said, past the Main Stage and then down another forest path to the Garden Stage. Let's go."

I crumple the map into my pocket and start speed-walking the trail. Shilo races to catch up, and we link arms like we always do.

As we approach the Main Stage area, the crowds thicken and the sounds of the festival stream right around me. The bass pounds through every bone. The high pitch of a flute pushes me forward. I'm glad for Shilo's arm as we are jostled between dancing kids with painted faces, some dressed in fairy clothes.

"Whoa." Shilo stops. "Check it out. It's Lunar! This must be their first performance."

On the Main Stage, framed by speakers and lights, the band is performing its latest big hit, the sound filling the sky.

"Wow, look how they move around on the stage," I say. "So not like us when we perform. These guys look like they're having fun."

The banjo player sidles up next to one of the fiddlers and gently hip-checks her. She laughs. I imagine myself right in that moment. Wishing we could listen and watch, I drag Shilo along.

A tune starts playing in my head, the familiar rhythm lifting me lightly through the crowd—the tune I hope will bring the judges to their feet and make them forget the last player. Ahead I can see a big sign with an arrow that says *Garden Stage*.

Shilo and I weave through a tangled mess of power cords to the mossy forest trail rimmed by giant evergreens. As we walk, the Main Stage sounds begin to fade. I sneak a peek behind me. No one.

"Let's run," I say. It's so quiet in the trees that all I hear is my breath and my feet crunching the gravel on the path. But then I hear, quietly at first, the sounds of a fiddle rocketing through the "Tam Lin" reel, a tune that makes you want to dance. Or fight. It's my tune. I stop running to listen. Each note is clear and perfect.

We reach a clearing full of people sprawled about on the grass. A small stage, built around the trees, seems like part of the forest. The guy we saw in the lineup is on the stage, playing my tune. I drop my fiddle case off my back with a thump.

"That's the one I was going to do," I hiss to Shilo.

He finishes the last note with a jump. The audience claps, and a few people even hoot. Then he bows so deep he almost seems to be mocking the crowd. His wavy dark hair just grazes his shoulders and swishes back and forth as he bows.

He walks to the edge of the stage, jumps off easily and keeps walking. I try not to stare as he joins a small group of musicians who all look older than him.

"He was pretty good," Shilo says. "You'll just have to come up with another tune. You're good at that."

I spot a table that looks official and march over.

"Hi," I say to a guy relaxing in a chair. "Can I still enter the contest?" My hands start to shake. The contest is the only plan I've got to show my mom how serious I am.

"Hi. Well, let's see. The cutoff for checking in was about fifteen minutes ago," he says. "But there's no one who really minds, you know what I mean?" I stare at him. I don't really know what he means. I wish Ms. O'Krancy were here to help. He looks at me. "Ah, why not? What's your name? I'll check the list."

"Rose Callaghan," I say. "And check for Shilo Scott as well." I watch as he scrolls down the list with one finger, moving about as fast as an inchworm. Out of the corner of my eye I see Shilo hovering.

"Murray's just about to go on!" she says. "How the heck did he get here so fast?"

We both turn to see Murray stepping onto the stage. He introduces himself, puts his fiddle under his chin and starts playing. He sounds pretty good. He plays "St. Anne's Reel," a really fast tune I wish I could choose.

I turn back to the desk. The registration guy is still searching for my name, flipping papers and making a giant mess of his table. I stuff my hands in my pockets to stop them from shaking. I need to win this contest. But to win I need to actually be in the contest.

"Here we go! I found both of you," he says. "You can go stand in line, stage left. You'll find out tomorrow who made the top twenty. And don't forget to cast your vote for People's Choice." He points to a big red box on the table with a pile of blank papers next to it.

Murray finishes up his tune. I leave Shilo clapping and walk straight to stage left. There are only a few performers in line to compete. I look out at the crowd. It's way bigger than I expected.

The next performer in line is struggling to tune her fiddle. She looks at me, then quickly focuses again on her tuning, biting her bottom lip. I feel as scared as she looks. I close my eyes and try to think of the perfect tune. I don't want to do one that was just played.

The girl in front of me heads onstage. I have only a few minutes left. Shilo is next in line behind me. The fiddler onstage drones out the ending to a slow tune, one that may have actually been written for a funeral. I hear some quiet, polite clapping. Then it's my turn. I walk up the stairs.

"I'm Rose Callaghan," I say as soon as I reach the microphone. I put on my best performance smile.

No hesitation. That's what my dad used to say. Thinking of my dad makes me realize I know just what to play. I lift my bow and start to fiddle. The notes of "Drowsy Maggie" storm out of my instrument. I tap my toe and move from side to side to feel the rhythm. The reel picks up speed like a downhill skier, snow flying, wind gusting. I can feel my bow arm aching to keep up. I forget the rush to get here. I forget the guy in the cap who played my tune. I just feel my fiddle under my chin, the warm sounds and vibrations flowing through me.

Five

After the contest Shilo and I sit on the grass next to the stage. The rush I got while I was performing has faded, and now all I can think about is whether I played the high B notes in tune. I was lucky I was able to come up with an alternative at the last second. I should have had more tunes in mind. It was dumb to be unprepared.

"You sounded good. You'll probably make it to the final round," Shilo says. "At least you didn't forget to play the second half of your tune, like I did. I don't think I have a chance."

"Hey." It's the guy in the cap. I sit up a bit straighter. "Nice tune. Tough one."

"Yours was also a tough one," I say.

"Yep," he says with a shrug. He slings his fiddle case onto his back and motions toward the path. "I'm Liam. You planning on grabbing some food at the dinner tent?"

"Uh, yeah, I was just about to head over there."

"Want some company?"

"Sure." I take my time putting my fiddle away so I don't seem flustered. I glance up and see him tapping a foot and swaying a bit to some private music in his head. I do that all the time too.

"I'm going to go see if I can find Murray," Shilo says to me, smiling. "I'll catch up with you later, okay?"

I grin back at her and then join Liam on the path. Close up he smells like spearmint.

"So you're Rose."

"Yep, I'm Rose. Am I wearing a name tag?"

"No," he says, laughing. He has a good smile. "I heard you introduce yourself onstage."

Okay. Right. He was listening.

"I love that tune you did," Liam says as we walk. "I wonder why they called it 'Drowsy Maggie' when it's so upbeat. No way you could sleep through that tune."

"Yeah, I like playing that one," I say. "I like all the string crossings."

"Do you remember when you first started playing, how it felt kind of awkward? My brain felt pulled in all directions, and my fingers wouldn't cooperate." He reaches up and adjusts his knitted cap. His jeans are faded, and the hole in the knee looks real, not like he bought pre-ripped jeans.

"I remember wanting to play like my dad," I say. "It looked like he wasn't even thinking. But I have to work hard to stay in tune, keep my bowing smooth and keep my brain from overheating."

"Totally—me too. Then one day I stopped thinking and just played." Liam gestures wildly with his hands, playing air violin. "Now I'm free. When I play the rest of the world disappears."

"When did you start playing?" I ask, slowing my steps so we can talk as long as possible.

"When I was a kid. Everyone in my family plays an instrument. It's just what you do. Fiddles were always hanging about, so that's where I started," Liam says. "Sounds like you lucked out with a dad who played too."

The thought of my dad makes my brain lurch to a stop, and I can't think of anything to say.

We walk in silence. I focus on placing my feet over the roots and rocks so I don't fall flat on my face. Liam softly sings a tune. I can't help but smile.

"Have you ever been to a real session?" he asks.

"I play all the time with my group," I reply.

"Yeah, but that's an organized group with a teacher telling you what and how to play." Liam adjusts his cap. "A session is where everyone sits in a circle, someone starts a tune and everyone who can or wants to plays. Some people do harmonies, some do melodies. There's lots of different instruments. It's real and in the moment. It's what Celtic music is based on." He pauses and turns to me. "I'm going to a late-night session tomorrow night."

I want to go. I have to go. But I don't want to act completely desperate. The sun has dipped low, and a hazy gold light shines through the trees. The evening suddenly feels full of possibility.

"How do you get invited?" I ask, trying to sound like I'm only considering.

"No invitation needed—it's open to all musicians. Are you a musician?" He looks at me and grins.

"Yeah, I'm a musician," I say. But my face flushes. I so want to be a real musician. "I just meant how did you hear about it?"

"I went to one on the very first night I arrived. Really cool. And you'd be surprised how much you'll learn from some of the old players if you just listen and don't play super loud," Liam says.

It seriously bugs me that he thinks he knows how I'll act. He just met me. And it bugs me even more because I know I probably *would* play loud. I like being heard.

As we approach the giant white meal tent, I can hear the sounds of dinner getting under way. People are chatting, and plates and cutlery clink.

I stop and turn to Liam. "Where do we meet?" I say.

He looks right at me. He has warm brown eyes.

"Nine o'clock. You see that big log right over there?" He nods toward a fallen tree covered with green moss and ferns. "I'll meet you just behind that."

"Okay, cool," I say, even though I'm thinking nine is pretty late.

Six

"Come on, I want to get a good spot." I steer Shilo through the Marketplace and toward our first music workshop. People dash in all directions. A woman with a guitar on her back and a baby on her front marches by me carrying a coffee and a waffle.

The workshop this morning is with one of my music idols, Robin Ross, a famous fiddler from Louisiana. Last week I spent a whole evening surfing around her website. She has a few albums, she headlines festivals, she teaches, she's famous. She's definitely serious about music. But not classical music.

"Over there—I see it." We head toward a squat wooden building with a big sign saying *Robin*

Ross—Cajun Fiddle. I hope we get a spot right at the front.

We scoot inside a large room with high, beamed ceilings. Sunlight pours through the windows.

"Come on in!" A woman wearing a snug orange sleeveless dress with funky-looking boots sits in a circle of mostly empty chairs. Her hair is in perfect ringlets. "Take a seat wherever you like." Her voice sounds like there's no hurry. "I've got some great tunes lined up for us to learn together."

I want to ask Robin so many questions about her music, her life, everything. Instead I say nothing. I feel like the words are stacked so tightly in my throat they can't escape.

We unpack and choose seats close to Robin. The circle fills quickly, and people start putting out a second circle of chairs behind the first one.

"You were right—I'm glad we got here early so we could get good seats," Shilo whispers as everyone gets settled. One woman starts to set up a music stand in front of her chair.

"Sorry, ma'am," Robin says. "Cajun music is an oral tradition—that means we learn by ear, and we don't use sheet music." The woman gets a bit red in the face but puts her stand away.

"All right, everyone, let's get started. I am Robin Ross. Welcome to my Cajun fiddle workshop. Some of you may know me, some of you may not." She smiles as she talks, and her ringlets bounce about. I sit frozen in my chair. I don't want to miss a word. "What I do know is that y'all are here so I can share some great tunes and fun facts—should we jump right in?"

"Woot!" Shilo calls out.

"Let's play!" says a voice just behind my chair. I swivel around to look. It's Liam. He's sprawled on his chair, a big smile on his face. I smile at him and then quickly twist back to face Robin. I glance at Shilo, and she's giving me a raised eyebrow. I try to ignore both of them and focus on Robin—I need to figure out how she became so successful. And I need her to recognize me as a promising player.

"Okay, I'll play the first couple of notes, and y'all play it back to me. We'll repeat that a few times until we've got it," Robin says. "I'll play the tune for you once first so you can hear it." She raises her fiddle and starts to play, bowing on more than one string at a time. Somehow it sounds like more than one fiddle playing.

I lean over to Shilo. "She's amazing! It sounds like she's accompanying herself, like she's her own band."

"I so want to learn how to do that," Shilo says.

When Robin finishes, everyone claps like she's just performed a full concert. "Okay, the trick with this one is that you need to play it kind of slippery. Picture yourself as a snake coiling 'round and 'round some thick tree branches." She demonstrates a few notes again. "You don't want to play it harsh, like a bunch of stomping trolls. Think light."

We learn the notes by listening to Robin play. We repeat it over and over. I can feel myself playing with gritted teeth and a clenched jaw as I will myself to learn the melody. I wish we had the music. I'm so much better when I can read the notes first.

"One more time! You guys are starting to sound great!"

Robin's energy is contagious. I can hear Liam playing behind me. He seems to have caught on to the whole melody already, and that makes me focus more. My brain slowly begins to release its death grip on the rest of my body, and my fingers take over, automatically going to the right strings, the right notes. I begin to relax, move my body and look around the room as I play.

"That sounded amazing, everyone," Robin says, leaning back in her chair with a satisfied sigh. "How did it make you feel?"

I shift in my chair, which suddenly seems hard as rock. I'm thinking of the perfect answer when Liam shouts out.

"Like climbing a mountain. While being chased by wolves!"

Everyone laughs. I can't help but smile as well.

"Nice. Yeah, I know what you mean. It makes me feel like I'm surfing big waves," Robin says. "Anybody have any questions?" A boy puts up his hand.

"She has a degree in folk music," Shilo whispers in my ear.

"I didn't know you could get a university degree in folk music!" I whisper back. My mom would certainly have an opinion on that.

"I once heard of someone who got their degree in puppet making. So anything's possible."

Behind me I can hear Liam plucking the melody we just learned. A woman asks Robin to check the tuning of her fiddle. I run my hand over the back of my fiddle, the smooth wood warm as usual.

"Hey." Liam leans forward between our chairs, a puzzled smile on his face. A few pieces of dark hair have escaped his cap.

"Hi," I say. "How's it going?"

"Do you know where the tune goes in the second phrase of the B part? I think I'm missing a note." He plucks the part, and I listen like it was the most important test of my life.

"Here...in this spot." He stops and looks at me.

"Oh, that goes up to the A," I say, trying to sound casual, but I'm not 100 percent sure. He tries it out, and it sounds right.

"Okay, yeah. I should have picked that up." He smiles all the way to his eyes.

"No problem," I say.

"Okay, everyone, thanks for your patience," Robin says. "Let's get back to playing some more tunes!"

"Thanks," Liam whispers. I give him one of my best smiles and then turn around to face the front again. Shilo pokes me on my toe with her bow. She knows I want to keep talking with Liam.

"Okay, let's learn another Cajun favorite of mine." Robin puts her fiddle under her chin. "I'll teach you the melody and then let's get some of you doing a harmony part. Let's give this one some southern swamp flavor, all right?"

We learn the melody and then Robin gets a few volunteers to play a simple harmony. This is exactly the type of music I want to learn.

"Great work, everyone! Sadly, our time is almost up." Robin stands, and everyone quiets down. "Since this is the first workshop of the festival, I'm supposed to share some news with y'all." She has my attention. "For those of you who participated in the first round of the fiddle contest yesterday, don't forget to check the information board."

I was so focused on the tunes, on trying to remember all the parts at once, that I forgot to worry about the contest!

"Results should be posted soon. Good luck to y'all."

Seven

"The results must be up already," Shilo says as we leave the workshop. "Look at the crowd!"

People are standing five deep on tippy-toes to see the notice taped to a huge slab of wood covered in papers. Shilo hops up and down. No way that will work.

"Come on," she says, pulling me into the crowd. I feel people filling the space behind me. Nervous energy pours off everyone like steaming water. People at the front turn and try to push back. Some look gleeful, and others look like someone stole their puppy.

I know it will be bad news. I played sloppy. And too slow. My name won't be up there.

Eventually Shilo and I make it to the front. And there is the list, a handwritten page.

Shilo puts her finger on the list and runs down the page. "There!" she shrieks. "You're in!"

I throw myself at the board, accidently elbowing the woman beside me. There it is—*Rose Callaghan.* I nod like an idiot. We turn and push our way back out.

"Wait, what about you?" I ask. I didn't see her name. Didn't even think of looking.

"I didn't make it." Shilo says this with a smile. But I know it must hurt.

"Oh, there's Emilia. I'm going to go see if she made the next round," Shilo adds.

"Hey, you look like you just got good news."

I turn around. Liam. I try to look cool about it, but I can't wipe off the giant grin plastered across my face.

"Yeah, I did," I say. "You?"

"Yep," he says, smiling. "Now the real fun begins."

"Totally," I reply.

"I saw a tent over in the Marketplace that was full of sheet music. It looked kind of cool," he says, swinging his fiddle case onto his back.

"Do you want to go check it out?" I blurt out the question before I have time to worry about whether he'll say yes.

"Yeah, let's do it," Liam says. "Does your friend want to come with us?" He looks at Shilo, who has wandered back over.

I'm also looking at Shilo, hard. I hope she is getting the message *no, you don't want to come.*

"I'm Shilo. Thanks, but...I promised Emilia I'd eat lunch with her," Shilo says quickly. "She didn't make the next round either. Let me know if you find anything good."

"All right. See ya, Shilo," Liam says and turns to leave.

I give Shilo a quick hug. "Thanks for under-standing," I whisper. She nods. I wish she had made the final round too.

I am about to join Liam but realize Robin Ross is standing right behind me. It's now or never.

"Excuse me, Robin?" I say. "I was just in your workshop. Could I ask you something?"

"Sure," she says. "But it will have to be quick. I've only got a minute."

"I'll be quick as lightning," I say, hoping that

sounds quirky not dorky. I see Liam behind her, watching us with a puzzled look on his face.

"Well, I remember you mentioning that you have a degree in music. And it doesn't seem like you're into classical music so..." I realize I'm not really sure what I want to ask her. "I...uh...I'm starting to think about what I'll do after high school. I think I want to study Celtic or folk music."

"That's fantastic! And I know just the place." She puts her fiddle case down. "It's called Berklee. Not Berkeley in San Francisco. People often get them confused. Berklee College of Music is in Boston and is considered one of the best places in the country to study contemporary music. I wasn't lucky enough to go there myself, but lots of my friends did. They offer programs in everything from jazz to rock to folk."

I feel something inside me light up. "You mean it's like a music university?"

"Absolutely!" She nods. "And I'm pretty sure they have summer camps for kids your age. Check out their website. Sorry, I have to get to my next workshop. But good luck!"

"Thanks," I say. As she walks away, I am thinking that Robin has given me the puzzle piece

I didn't even know was missing. Berklee sounds perfect. Maybe there actually is a way for me to follow my dreams *and* keep my mom happy.

Eight

iam and I make our way down the path to the Marketplace. An intoxicating smell of Indian curry and sweet greasy pastry makes my stomach rumble. I hope Liam can't hear it.

"I know I said music tent, but I'm pretty hungry," Liam says. "Want to get some grub?"

"Sure," I say, because I'm starving too. We veer toward the food tents.

"Falafels?" I suggest, nodding toward a Lebanese food tent.

"No way." He smiles. "We have to go all out." He scans the tents. He looks serious, like he's on an important mission.

"Okay, how about mini donuts?" I say. "Deliciously greasy and nutrition-free. Plus covered in sugar."

"Perfect." He smiles his crinkly smile again.

We leave the tent with a warm bag of donuts and plop down on the grass next to a circle of musicians strumming mandolins. I reach into the bag and grab a donut. I pop the whole thing in my mouth. It's so hot it almost burns my tongue, but the sweet sugar and cinnamon taste like summer.

I steal glances at Liam when he's not looking. He keeps his cap on even in the heat. His head must be hot. I want to ask so many questions. Where is he from? Did he come here with anyone? But I like the feeling of sitting in silence with an almost complete stranger. It feels right and weird at the same time.

We get through the bag of donuts in no time.

"Music tent?" Liam asks.

"I'm in," I say. Along the way we pass bongo drums, a tent filled with jewelry made from seashells and rough twine, and a tent advertising *Special Tea*. It's so crowded now, it feels like I'm stuck in an ant hill.

"Here." Liam nods toward a white tent where blue milk crates are stuffed with sheets of music. "This should keep us entertained for a while." He grins.

"Do you think these are sorted somehow?" I say, looking at the jumble of papers. It looks like my dad's filing system. Everything piled in a mysterious way only he would understand.

"Well, so far I've seen some Hungarian dances, some Finnish polkas and a Scottish jig," Liam says. "A bit random."

I flip through a few sheets. Some are crisp and new, but others are crumpled and stained, like they've been sitting in the bottom of a box for a hundred years.

"I like trying to figure out what the tune is about," says Liam, not even looking up from his intent flipping. "My teacher back home likes to tell random bits of stories. I never really knew if she was making them up or not. Did you know that the Irish folk song 'Sí Bheag, Sí Mhór' is about big and little fairy hills?"

"Really? Cool. Did you ever play around with 'Old Joe Clark,' making up even crazier lyrics?"

"Totally," he says. We both get back to flipping through sheets. I can't stop smiling.

After a while I can't keep all my questions blocked up inside. "Where's home anyway?"

I ask, dusting my hands off and standing up.

"Back east," he says, like the east coast is some quaint town and not thousands of places. "But we just moved to Calgary. That's where my folks were able to find work."

"Oh." I nod. Moving sounds scary. I wonder if he finds it easy to make new friends. "Are you performing tonight?"

"Just a sec. I'm going to buy this sheet. It's a crazy-looking polka my dad will love."

We join the lineup at the front of the tent, where a grizzled little man sits in an old-fashioned wooden school desk. He hands out change from a beat-up cookie tin. Liam turns around to answer my question.

"I'm not performing tonight. I'm not here with a group."

"You came by yourself?" Interesting.

"I did," he says. "But my family totally supports me, which is awesome, since it's kind of a big deal to come all the way across the mountains."

"How did you get here?" The man is carefully counting out nickels and dimes.

"Took a Greyhound bus. I busked at stops along the way for money." I picture him standing at a busy bus terminal, his case open and filled with change. My mom would never have let me take the bus alone. Taking the airplane from Vancouver with my group had been a pretty big deal.

Liam finally gets to the front of the line and pays for his music. "Do you have to be somewhere now?" he asks. "We've got some time before dinner."

"I wouldn't mind checking out some other parts of the festival," I say. I also wouldn't mind walking through the crowds with him some more.

"There are tons of small stages," Liam says, rising up on his toes to see over a pack of teenagers in front of us. They are all carrying cello cases like backpacks, making them about seven feet tall. "I can see one that way."

"Let's go," I say. I should head back to practice my performance tunes with Shilo. But I know the tunes backward and forward. I like that this day with Liam feels as if it will never end. We stop and listen to a trio on guitar, double bass and fiddle. The bass player keeps his eyes shut but moves his whole body as he plays.

"I love how everyone here is so into their music," Liam says. "I feel like this is where I'm supposed to be."

"Me too," I say. I only wish my mom could see that this is where I belong.

We stroll through the tents of the Marketplace and onto yet another winding path through the trees. We come across a dozen or so small kids sitting on rocks covered with soft moss, playing a familiar reel. I smile, because not too long ago I was one of them. Squeaking just out of tune, pressing too hard on the strings, but feeling like a superhero. I look over at Liam. He's also smiling.

We walk for a few minutes more and discover a huge vegetable garden bordered by a rough stone wall just high enough for us to sit on.

The music of the tiny fiddlers plays in the background, like chickadees singing. Liam and I settle on the stone wall. It feels warmed by the sun.

A young woman walks by carrying a huge bin of freshly dug carrots. "I might see if they're looking for a farm intern," Liam says, watching the girl walk away. "I could stay a while."

"You want to stay here? What about home, school?" I ask.

"I don't know. It would be something different. My family would be happy if I went to college, but they can't help me pay for it. So I might try some other stuff first." He looks at me. "What do you want to do?"

I want to tell him my dreams of touring and being a Celtic musician. But they sound silly now. There are so many musicians just at this one camp. I didn't realize how many people might share my dream.

"I'm not sure," I say, watching a sprinkler wave back and forth across the vegetables.

"I want to try everything I can," he says. "Like the farming thing. I figure, why not?"

I don't want to think about this anymore. I open up my fiddle case, the zipper making a familiar, satisfying sound.

Liam snaps open his case. "Pretty crap case, hey?" he says, pulling out his fiddle. The wood is so dark it's almost black. "But I love it. It's been in my family for ages."

"Yeah, I know what you mean," I say. "This fiddle was my dad's." I gently touch the smooth wood.

"Can I see it?" Liam asks, setting his own fiddle down and stretching out his hands.

"Sure," I say, but I'm a bit reluctant. I don't like handing it over to anyone. He takes the fiddle gently and touches the wood just like I did.

"Want to play mine for a tune and I'll play yours?" he asks. "Something slow." The mini donuts pitch around in my stomach. I don't know how I feel about someone else playing my dad's fiddle.

"Okay, but just one tune," I say. Liam holds my fiddle with one solid, large hand. I notice several bracelets of dark beads on his wrist. With his other hand he picks up his fiddle and passes it to me. It feels completely different but somehow the same as mine. I lift it to my chin and my fingers know what to do.

"Let's play 'Skye Boat,'" I say.

"Simple and classic," he replies. "Can't go wrong." The melody is slow and beautiful and makes me think of searching for something. Liam's fiddle has a dark, rich tone that surprises me. And I like hearing the bright tones of my own fiddle as he plays it.

His fingers are long, and he moves them across the fingerboard with such ease. I'm impressed. He counters my melody with long, beautiful harmony notes.

"Nice fiddle," he says when we finish.

"Yeah, I like it," I say. "My dad gave it to me."

"He's not around anymore?"

I can't bring myself to look at him or answer. I just nod.

"Sorry. I didn't mean to pry."

I nod again, not trusting myself to speak.

"I can't imagine what that must be like so I won't try to," he says. "I know I'm lucky to have my whole family. And yeah, I love that my fiddle has been in my family pretty much forever. A great-great-great-uncle brought it with him when he sailed here from Scotland. He played down below on the journey."

I'm so relieved Liam didn't ask me a million stupid questions about my dad. Usually people force me to talk about it and go on and on about how sorry they are.

"Okay, I have to get going," Liam says, handing me back my fiddle. "I have to do some prep for my performance tomorrow." I must look confused, because Liam explains, "Yeah, I...uh...I won the People's Choice."

How could he forget to mention that? "Oh," I say. And then after a beat I add, "That's great!"

Actually, I'm not sure how I feel. I am happy for him, but I wanted to win.

"Yeah, it will be great to have a few friendly faces in the audience. If you can, come by and listen." He puts his fiddle back in his case. "Oh, and I wanted to ask—"

I have a crazy thought that he's going to ask me to do a duet with him as part of his performance. Maybe we could do "Skye Boat," just like we did now.

"—are you still game for the session tonight?"

"Definitely." I slowly put my own fiddle away. I'm glad Liam couldn't hear my dumb thoughts.

"Great." Liam heads down the path, then turns and calls out, "Thanks, Rose. This was a good day."

Nine

The evening drags on. Shilo and I eat dinner in the food tent. I wonder how Liam's performance prep is going. "I can't believe how long it took him to tell me he won the People's Choice. No way I could have waited all day," I say.

"You definitely could not have kept that secret," Shilo says, laughing. I'm still imagining Liam and me playing together. Like the picture on the festival website.

"Hi, girls." A voice shatters my duet dream. Shilo's mom approaches our table. "I wanted to let you know that I'm volunteering at the variety show this evening. I won't be back until late, so make sure you get to bed early tonight, okay?" Without waiting for a reply, she takes off.

I think about Liam's invitation and our plan to meet at nine. Maybe the variety show will go later than the session. But what if Anna comes home early and I'm not there? I need Shilo's help.

After dinner, on our way to group rehearsal, I work up the nerve to talk to her about it. "I have a big favor to ask of you," I say. "I need to stay out late tonight."

Shilo gives me a bug-eyed look before she answers. "Why? Where are you going?"

"Liam asked me to go to a session with him," I say. "That's when musicians get together to play tunes."

"Oh!" Shilo says.

"I would invite you as well, but how can we both go?" I say. "It starts after curfew." I know that sounds lame.

"What? You're going to get in trouble," she says.

"Not if you cover for me," I say. If Shilo agrees, maybe one day I can return the favor. "We could come up with something really good. Then, if your mom does find out, she won't even know you were covering for me. Please!"

"Okay, fine," she says. "But don't get caught."

"Do you think your mom would believe I was sick and went to the first-aid tent after rehearsal?"

"I don't know," Shilo says. "You never get sick. Maybe if she gets home before you do I'll tell her we were late coming back from rehearsal and you were right behind me. You stopped to talk to someone you met at our workshop. Maybe Robin Ross. But you should only stay a little while. Like half an hour."

"Thanks! You are the best," I say, giving her a hug.

Our two-hour rehearsal feels more like a week-long math class. Finally we finish, and I run ahead of everyone back to my yurt. I peer once into the tiny, dirty mirror above the small table between our beds. In this heat my head is a frizzy mess. I twist and scoop my hair into a half pony-tail. It will have to do.

As I make my way to the meeting spot, daylight fades into inky dusk. The path feels deserted. The trees start to look like dark hands about to reach out and grab me. I stumble on a root. I cry out, then keep going at a slower pace. I don't know what time it is. I hope he'll wait for me.

Ten

I am relieved to see Liam sitting on the log, strumming his fiddle.

"I knew you'd come," he says with a smile. He gets up and we walk to a round, white canvas building that looks like it has a tree growing out of the roof. Glass front doors and a circle of windows flood warm light into the dark night.

"Will there be room for us?" I ask, then wish I hadn't. Probably a dumb question.

"Sure," Liam answers. "Musicians never get turned away from a session. We just make room." He bounds up the three stairs and pushes open the doors without knocking. I'm happy to let him go first. As I enter, I see worn wooden floors covered with black instrument cases. In the middle of the room a giant tree trunk, bark grizzled and worn, reaches up and through the roof.

Musicians sit in a circle of wooden chairs. Most hold fiddles, but I also see three guitars, a ukulele and a couple of flutes. Two cello players sit next to each other, talking excitedly. A girl about my age with long blond hair and glasses tunes a harp in the corner. I spot a few empty chairs and want to grab two of them right away so Liam and I can sit next to each other.

"Liam! You brought a friend!" A girl with short spiky hair, holding an Irish drum, waves at us.

"Hi, Sara. Rose, this is Sara. She's always trying to push the fiddles faster with her drumbeats," Liam says, smiling. "She thinks we're all too slow. Don't worry—Rose knows how to keep the pace moving. You should have seen her tearing up the stage yesterday with 'Drowsy Maggie.'" I smile. Liam's comment brings back some of the warmth I felt as I played the reel.

"Oh yeah?" Sara says. "Welcome, Rose." Sara seems so confident, even though she's not much older than me.

"Thank you," I squeak, trying to reclaim my lost voice. I take my fiddle out and tuck it under my right arm. In such a crowded space, I'm terrified it will get damaged if I put it down.

"Okay, everyone, let's get started," Sara calls out above all the chatter and random notes. "People will keep trickling in, but let's play. Why don't we start with 'Mairi's Wedding' to loosen up?"

Liam and I stand behind the circle of chairs. We missed out on grabbing seats.

"Do you know the tune?" I ask Liam, my voice low. No one has music stands.

He taps his foot. "Yep, it's a standard. I bet you've played this one even if you don't know it by name."

"Sure, yeah," I say, trying to sound confident. I'll figure it out. I'll tear it up.

"Okay, it's in the key of D," Sara calls out, tapping her drum in a steady beat. "I'll give you one bar to start. Try to keep up as best you can."

My brain runs through all the tunes we've learned in the Celtic group. Maybe I do know this one. I place my bow on my D string and hope that's where it starts.

"One, two, three, four," Sara calls out. The room erupts in sound as we rip through the first few bars of music. I don't recognize the tune, but I like it. It's cheerful and up-tempo.

One of the best skills my classical violin teacher has taught me is the art of the fake. She said all musicians do it sometimes. There is no shame, she insists. I move my bow back and forth across my open D string. I try to mimic the fingering of the fiddler seated in front of me.

I look over at Liam. He's bobbing his head and swaying from side to side. I can hear him loud and clear. I hope he doesn't notice that at this moment I'm a total faker. I watch his fingers as we move into the second time through the tune. Folk tunes are short and are usually played at least three times through, often more. The second time around I catch a few riffs and manage to play along. I feel awkward, but I keep my foot tapping. I can't quite put together some of the phrases, so it all feels separate to me, not quite right.

The second half of the tune goes to the E string, and this time I catch a section of the melody. I feel part of the group for a few moments. Then I'm lost again. But by the third time through, the tune starts to click, and my fingers reach for the notes before my brain can overthink.

"Let's pick up the pace for the last time through!" Sara yells above the music. Around me the room hums and moves. Sara's drum and the deep cello bass line drive the fiddles forward, urging and pushing, like there's a race somewhere or a party to get to. The melody line jumps above the harmony, wanting to be noticed.

I try to keep up, but I haven't quite got the tune and fall back to faking. I keep my face composed and move my fingers and bow to match people, but I'm all wrong and I hope Liam doesn't notice.

"Awesome, hey?" says Liam once the tune is over.

Sara announces the next tune. I don't know it either, so I'm back to faking. Liam looks so relaxed. So does everyone else. I wish I could have had a set list. And I wish I had a watch so I could keep an eye on the time. I don't know how late Shilo's mom will stay out. I'm jammed into the circle, with another line of fiddle players standing behind me. We start yet another tune I don't know. I'm going to be in big trouble.

Eleven

Moonlight guides me along the dark path. Liam was chatting to Sara after the session ended, and I didn't want to stick around. When I reach the yurt I share with Shilo and Anna, it's all lit up. Through the window, I can see Anna pacing.

"Uh-oh," I mutter. Maybe I can say I got lost in the woods. I take a deep breath, walk up the stair onto our yurt platform and grab the worn wooden handle. I pause for a second before I push it open.

"Thank goodness!" Anna cries. I squint in the bright light. Anna rushes over and wraps herself around me. Over her shoulder I can see Shilo on her camp bed, her head propped up on an elbow. She has a weird look on her face.

"I was so worried," Anna says, squeezing me. I feel a bit light-headed from her hug and wish I could sit down. She backs away, drops into the one battered wooden chair we have and flicks her sandals off. "I have the whole festival security team out looking for you."

I look over at Shilo for some backup, but now she's staring up at some really exciting spot on the ceiling.

"Sorry, I ran into Robin Ross after our rehearsal, and then after that I guess I wasn't paying attention to the time..." I walk over to my own bed, drop my fiddle case, pop my shoes off and curl my legs up. Nothing I can think of will work. Fell in a creek? Not wet. Witnessed a heart attack and had to run for medical assistance? Got lost? They all sound ridiculous.

"Rose." Anna interrupts my thoughts. She is massaging her temples, her head bent forward. "You've been missing for more than two hours." She looks at me. "I am willing to listen if you want to tell me the truth about where you've been."

The silence lasts for what seems like forever. Shilo won't even look at me. Anna has dropped her head and is massaging her temples again.

"Okay, this is the truth. I heard about a Celtic music session happening after our rehearsal," I say. No need to mention Liam. "I'm sorry. I couldn't ask you because you were busy volunteering." I feel a bit bad as soon as I say this, but I was scrambling. "I thought I would only be a little while." I shift a bit on my bed, and it creaks. I feel cornered in this silent room.

"I saw you tonight at the meal tent. You could have asked me then, although I still would have said no. The fact is, you broke curfew, so as your official chaperone I have to play by Ms. O'Krancy's rules. So tomorrow you will not participate in any performances or workshops. And you are banned from all parts of the festival except the yurt, the outhouses and the meal tent." She sighs loudly and shakes her head. "I am sorry to have to do this. I know how much being here means to you. But you should have thought of the consequences before breaking the rules."

"But our group performance is tomorrow night!" I say. "Please, please, please let me do the performance. I've been working for two years for this. I'll gladly miss everything else tomorrow."

I can't believe this is happening. My light-headed feeling isn't going away.

Anna looks sad. "You are definitely not attending any workshops or any other part of the festival tomorrow." She pauses. "But I will talk to Ms. O'Krancy about the evening performance, as I don't want your behavior to affect your entire group. No promises. She may very well ship you right home."

Anna stands up and slides her sandals on. "I have to go talk to security and let them know you've shown up. Get ready for bed. It's almost midnight." She heads out, the door shutting behind her with a bang.

I exhale and look over at Shilo. "Ugh, this sucks. Sorry I took so long. But it was hard to leave—I was all jammed in."

Shilo flips around on her bed so she's facing away from me and pulls her covers up.

"Shilo, what's up?" I know she's mad, but I need someone to talk to.

Shilo reaches out and flips off the only overhead light. I'm left sitting in the dark.

I pull my own covers up, not bothering with pajamas. In the dark and the silence, the tears come. I let them run down my cheeks and try not to sniffle. I hate myself for getting Shilo in trouble. What will my mom do when she hears how I screwed up?

I close my eyes and think back to all the faking I did tonight. I never realized how hard it is to learn tunes on the spot. My dad did it all the time and made it look so easy. What if I'm really not good enough to become a professional musician? Then what?

Twelve

I almost miss out on the performance. I sit around by myself all day, banned from everything. Including watching Liam play his People's Choice performance at the Marketplace stage. If only I had made it back before Anna did. If only I had just asked Anna if I could go to the session. Maybe she would have said yes. Then instead of being stuck here, I'd be watching Liam play. To distract myself, I practice the Cajun tune Robin Ross taught us yesterday. I play until my fingers cramp, but I still can't remember the whole melody.

It isn't until after dinner that Ms. O'Krancy decides to let me join the performance, but only for the good of the group. Anna called my mom but didn't get hold of her.

Now our fiddle group stands on the stage built into the trees. The audience sits below us on the grass. We are lit by real stage lights. I can feel the energy and warmth of the audience being drawn into our tunes. Feet stomp, and hands clap.

Our tunes are a part of me, as much as my fingers, my heart. My feet tap on the rough wooden floor of the stage. Each note flows crisp and bright from my dad's fiddle. I concentrate on my bow strokes, flowing some notes together with long slurs. Other times my bow attacks the strings. Shilo is with me on every note, every bow stroke. We imagined this night so many times. If only she was talking to me. I can feel her silence.

My hands start to shake as I lose focus, thinking about how I messed up last night. My bow starts to quiver on the string. I press the bow too hard, and my notes come out biting and creaky. I miss a count and am offbeat for a bar. I start to panic and then cringe as my pinky finger comes short for a high note and I'm out of tune, like a little kid. I try to keep breathing normally. I can't mess this up.

We finish our set of three jigs. Ms. O'Krancy, accompanying us on the guitar, starts a blistering fast reel. She used to tour the country with a folk band so knows how to get a crowd going. I shut my eyes for just one second to feel my fiddle vibrating in my hands and hear a *snap!*

My A string has broken. It's ridiculous to try to play without it. But I don't want to embarrass myself, not now. I pretend to play, but heat rises to my face. More faking. Just like at the session.

The last tune of the set feels like it's happening in slow motion. My ears are probably the color of bright red apples. Finally it ends. I bow with shame. I show my fiddle to Ms. O'Krancy and then slink off the stage to the storage area near the back.

I don't want to miss more than one set. I race to the table with the instrument cases, fling my case open and grab the extra strings I keep in the top pocket. I can hear stomping onstage as the group starts another set of reels. I sit down and place my fiddle between my legs, untwist the shards of the broken string and start winding the new string on the scroll.

I'm winding too fast, and the string refuses to lie flat. I hear Shilo start her flute solo. I have less than one minute to make it back onstage for the final set. What am I going to do? I glance up and see our group's spare fiddle. I hate the spare fiddle. It's practically made of plywood. I want to play my dad's fiddle. But then I imagine the group taking the final bow without me. I put my fiddle on top of a pile of cases and grab the spare fiddle. The wood feels cold.

As I walk back out onstage, Shilo is just finishing her solo on the Irish flute. The audience is silent. The high melody rings through the night, filling the forest and floating up to the sky. I tiptoe through the group to my place in the front. The stage lights almost blind me. I turn to watch Shilo. Her eyes are closed while she plays. I know she is nervous. I smooth my hand along the spare fiddle. It feels rough compared to mine. Ms. O'Krancy signals to us to get ready as Shilo plays her last note, long and sweet.

On the first note of the reel, I cringe. It sounds like I'm playing through an ancient record player, all static and noise. I push harder on the strings, hoping my energy will somehow bring beautiful sound to the fiddle. No luck. And then we're done. I grab Shilo's hand on one side of me and Murray's on the other, and we bow together, all of us. We stand up straight again and all file off the stage to the back.

"Nice solo, Shilo!" Emilia runs up and hugs Shilo. I want to say the same, do the same. I wanted to give Shilo the first hug.

"Rose, what happened to your fiddle?" Emilia asks.

"String broke," I say. "No big deal. I grabbed the spare fiddle because I was having trouble with the new A string. I'm going to go fix it now." I walk over to where I left my fiddle. It's not there.

"Hey, has anyone seen my fiddle?" Everyone is busy reliving the performance, note by note. "I thought I left it sitting on top of the cases on the table."

"Well, that was dumb," Emilia says. "That's not a safe place to leave it."

"I was kind of in a rush," I say, my cheeks hot. "You needed me out there. You can barely keep up."

"Okay, girls, that's enough." Ms. O'Krancy steps in between us. "Rose, are you sure that's where you left it? Take a look around."

I lean over the edge of the stage, and there it is on the ground, several feet away from the table.

"No," I breathe. It can't be. I hop down and pick it up. I turn it over, my heart thudding faster than our last reel. There's a giant crack all the way down the back. My dad's fiddle is ruined.

Thirteen

I wake the next morning to the sound of a slow, sad cello. I sit up and hug my legs. I'm alone in the yurt. My stomach grumbles to tell me it's way past breakfast. Beside my bed lies my fiddle case with my cracked fiddle. Shilo won't speak to me. I feel like a failure. I can't even change a string, let alone play like a real Celtic musician.

I reach out and fumble in my case for the photo of my mom and dad playing music. Mom looks so happy in the photo, her face bright and fresh. I have so many questions. Why doesn't she play the flute anymore? If Dad were still around, would he have come to the festival with me? Would Mom have joined us? Everything could have been so different.

"Argh," I say out loud to no one. I dress quickly and then look out the window. All I can see is a big fat crow picking at a brown apple on the ground. No people. The cello drones on from another yurt. I'm allowed to go to workshops today. There's a bluegrass jam that I really want to check out. But first I need to find Shilo.

I open the door. Outside, it's just me and the crow. As I walk past, the crow looks up at me and caws loudly.

"Yeah, I imagine I'm making you mad too." I say. "I'm good at that."

I walk past the other yurts, their porches draped with towels and random clothes.

My thoughts are bouncing around like popcorn. Only Shilo can really understand how gutted I am about my fiddle. And right now she hates me because I got her in trouble. Being shut out by Shilo makes everything that's happening even worse. I need to find a way to make things right between us again.

I see the huge wooden information board with the festival schedules and results tacked on it. Shilo was taking the Fabulous Flutes workshop before lunch, so I scan the board for the location and time. It ends at eleven thirty on the far side of the biggest meadow.

I veer across the meadow, my feet squelching in the damp grass. A hummingbird buzzes the wildflowers. I hear the beautiful high notes from the flutes floating above all the other sounds. As I get closer I see Shilo sitting in a chair at the front of an open-air tent, her legs crossed, feet bare.

I lean against a nearby stone wall and nest in between huge sunflowers to wait. My toe taps out the beat of the flute's tune. What if Shilo already told Emilia about what I did? Emilia won't stand up for me—she wants Shilo to be her best friend.

The workshop ends and I watch Shilo pack up her flute and start walking toward me. She's smiling. But as soon as she sees me the smile vanishes.

"Hi," I say quietly. She stops a few feet away, arms crossed. Her mouth is set. "How was your workshop?"

"You can't pretend that nothing happened," she says. "You got me in trouble." Her voice trembles. "Obviously you only care about yourself."

"That is not true," I say. I don't want to lose my best friend. I want us to keep playing music together. "I need to talk to you. I hate us being mad at each other." But the words *I'm sorry* are still jammed down at the base of my throat.

Shilo bites her lip. "Okay, fine, let's talk," she says. "Let's go this way. I have an idea."

I feel my jaw unclench. I let her lead me past a greenhouse and over to a huge wooden swing set. We each jump on a swing and start pumping our legs. It's silent except for the squeak of the metal hangers as we swing back and forth.

"The swings were always my favorite," Shilo says. A good sign. She's talking to me.

"What about the monkey bars?" I counter. "Remember how we used to climb on top of them so we could look down at the rest of the playground?"

She swings back and forth a few times before answering.

"I was looking up, Rose, not down."

I swallow, considering what she means. "You think I think I'm better than everyone else," I say. This is not where I wanted this conversation to go. I can feel my insides coiling up as I get ready to defend myself.

"Don't act surprised," Shilo says quietly. "You do like to be the leader. And sometimes you act like you can do whatever you want. But the other night you got me in trouble. My mom was sure I knew where you were, and she was really mad. You can't do whatever you want and expect me to just follow along like an idiot." Her quiet voice worries me. "You could at least say you're sorry. I'm supposed to be your best friend." Her voice cracks, and she won't look at me.

I feel small and rotten for letting her down. We swing for a few minutes that feel like hours. I think back to when my dad died. How Shilo sat with me in my room for days, curled up on my carpet, listening to music. She never forced me to talk. I have to apologize.

"You're right," I hear myself say finally. "I'm sorry that I lied, got you to cover for me and then didn't come back. I feel really terrible about getting you into trouble."

Shilo leaps out of her swing and lands on the grass, taking a few big steps to steady herself. I do the same, flinging myself out of the swing. She wraps herself around me in a big Shilo bear hug.

"Forgiven," she whispers. "I don't want to fight. I want to have fun with you. But you had to say sorry. And you'd better not leave me out or get me in trouble again."

I hug her back fiercely. "I won't. I promise," I say. "But tell me what I missed."

We settle down again on our swings.

"Okay, well, I was really mad at you," she says, leaning her body back so that her long hair brushes the ground as she swings low. "I was so excited about us hanging out together at this festival. But you took off with Liam. And then you showed up so late after the session. My mom was freaking out."

"I know." I lean back hard, pumping myself up higher. "I really am sorry."

"It has been awful not being able to tell you everything that's been going on," Shilo says. "Like, yesterday I ran into Murray and we walked to a harmony workshop together." I can see her face getting pink even as she swings by me. "It's so cool that he plays so many instruments. And he's so relaxed."

I really want to ask if they went to Liam's performance. Instead I say, "Did you make plans with him for later?" I let myself slowly glide to a stop.

"No," she moans, her shoulders lurching forward along with her hair. "I should have tried, but honestly, I was worrying about you and couldn't get the words out."

"You'll get another chance," I say, feeling terrible again. "I'll help you."

"So what happened? Why did it take you so long to get back the other night?" Shilo asks.

"It was crazy," I start, relieved to finally tell someone. "The room was packed with people, and I didn't know most of the tunes. I tried to figure some out, but I was faking it most of the time. I felt really dumb."

"There's millions of tunes," Shilo says. "You can't know them all."

She's right. But I want to be the musician people notice, the one improvising and playing in a higher octave. Not the clumsy girl figuring out the notes and playing on open strings.

"I know," I say, launching myself off the swing. "There's so much I need to figure out today. But first, let's get something to eat. I'm starving!"

Fourteen

S hilo and I eat lunch in the performers'
meal tent. I'm so hungry I barely taste the
hummus, pita and carrots. Outside, the sky
has turned gray.

"I need a plan fast," I say as we take our dishes
to the cleaning station, swirl them around in the
hot, soapy water, then walk outside. "There are
only two days left until the final round of the fiddle
contest. I need to get my fiddle fixed, and we need
to practice our tunes." A drop of water hits my nose.
Then another. People around us start scurrying.

"Let's go," Shilo says. "I don't want my flute
case to get wet." Rain splatters down, soaking our
hair and clothes. We run to our yurt and fling
the door open. It smells like a hot, wet bus full
of people.

"Since we're stuck here, we might as well practice," Shilo says, curling up on her bed after we've changed into dry clothes. She grabs her worn copy of the Irish music book that everyone uses, *O'Neill's Music of Ireland.* "You want to be ready."

Shilo's words remind me that she didn't make the final round. "Wait, you don't need to stick with me," I say. "You can go to another workshop or something. Find Murray."

Shilo shrugs. "I like hanging out with you. It's cozy in here—except for the smell." She smiles.

I don't know what I would have done if she was still mad at me. "I really have to get my fiddle fixed," I say, tucking my bare feet under my sleeping bag. I picture the horrible crack in the fiddle. What if it's never the same again?

"Even if there was a way, I really don't think we can go out in this rain." Shilo tucks her feet under the covers. Rain drums on the yurt wall. "What tunes are you doing in the contest?" she says, sitting up and flipping through the pages of the book.

"I'm not sure. What are the contest rules again?" I ask. I want to make sure I know exactly what to do for the contest. I can't mess up. Again.

Shilo rummages through her backpack and pulls out the crumpled page from the registration package. "Here. *Contestants will be asked to play three tunes in the final: a hoedown (breakdown, reel or hornpipe), a waltz and a tune of choice.* Okay, I'd stick with Irish tunes. So pretty."

I watch a moth fly frantically from light to light like it has no idea what to do or which way to go. I know how it feels. I wonder what tunes my dad would pick. Whenever I would play a new tune I'd learned from my teacher, he would pick up his fiddle—now my fiddle—and join in. He knew them all.

I realize I'm clenching my jaw so hard that my head hurts. "This is ridiculous. There's no way I can get my fiddle repaired by tomorrow since we're stuck here in a rainstorm." I picture Liam showing up to the contest with his beautiful dark fiddle under his arm, his tunes all prepared and ready to go. Me with a crappy spare fiddle and unprepared because I can't seem to focus.

Shilo nods. We both sit on her bed in silence for a minute, the only sound the slight buzz from the fluorescent lights. "I know you're bummed. But for now, can't we play some tunes? The spare fiddle might suck, but you don't." She looks over at me, a sad half smile on her face. I bite my lip so I don't cry.

My thoughts race around and around. Only playing music will stop them. Even on the sucky might-as-well-be-plywood spare fiddle. "Let's play," I say.

I have just tuned up when Anna walks in.

"Mom." Shilo looks startled to see her. "What are you doing here? Aren't you supposed to be at the festival store?"

"I found someone to take over for a few hours." She sits down on her bed with a sigh and looks pointedly at me. "I came back to give Rose a message."

I sit up straighter. Maybe she found a way to get my fiddle fixed.

"I left a message for your mom to let her know you broke curfew and we had to search for you. She just called back. She's coming to the festival the day after tomorrow. That's the earliest she can get away."

"What? Why?" I imagine my mom arriving, her navy suit pressed, her hair sleek. "I know I let you down, but I'm sorry."

Anna crosses her arms. "I know, but your mom just said she's coming. You'll have to talk to her."

Hot tears form in my eyes, but I quickly wipe them away. "Fine," I say. My mom will show up mad at me for breaking curfew. And then I picture the look of distaste on her face when she sees Dad's fiddle, destroyed. I have to get his fiddle fixed before my mom arrives. And I have to win the fiddle contest. It's the only way to show my mom I'm serious about music. That I'm good.

Fifteen

I wake to the shrieking of crows. Yurts are not soundproof.

"Argh," Shilo moans. "What are they doing? It sounds like every crow in the area is having a full-on screaming match right above us." She clutches her pillow over her head. Anna has already left for an early volunteer shift.

"It's like the rain last night. Everything bad has to happen while we're at this festival," I say. "Of course crows are going to wake us up. Next, I'll walk outside and probably get pooped on by a seagull."

"And then all the outhouses will back up and we'll have to do our business in the woods," Shilo says from under her pillow.

"And the meal tent will serve that lentil stew from yesterday for every meal for the rest of the week, including breakfast."

"Ewww!" Shilo squeals and pops out from under her pillow, smiling now. "Okay, that's yucky. Makes the crows seem like a beautiful sound to wake up to."

Our silly conversation makes me forget for a moment that today is the last day before the final contest round. My fiddle is cracked. Unplayable. My mom is on her way.

"Someone's got to be able to repair my fiddle," I say from under the covers. "It probably just needs some glue and varnish."

"I think we should ask Murray for help," Shilo says.

"You're just saying that because you like him."

"I do, but that's not why," she replies.

"Okay, why then?" I slowly sit up.

"His mom plays violin in the orchestra," she says, brushing her long hair out as she talks. I watch, mesmerized, as she untangles a giant knot. I would never have the patience to look after such long hair. "He might know something about getting instruments repaired."

Probably couldn't hurt to get some advice. "Okay, let's give it a try," I say. "Do you happen to know where we might find Murray?" I'm teasing her, and she knows it.

"Yes, yes, I do," Shilo says with a smile.

Outside, the air is cool, but last night's clouds have vanished. We walk in silence through the maze of yurts. Performers are quietly waking up. The sinks next to the outhouses have a six-deep lineup of girls carrying their toiletry bags.

"Zombies in pajamas," Shilo whispers to me. I don't say anything. I am trying not to get my hopes up. She links her arm with mine. "Okay, it's the last one on that row," she says, pointing to a yurt. "There."

I march up to the door and knock. Not a polite knock. More of a this-is-the-police-let-me-in type of knock. I turn around and see Shilo behind me, a nervous smile on her face. "You so like him," I say and turn back around. The door opens.

Mark, one of the other fiddlers in our group, stands in front of us wearing a fleece onesie covered with blue penguins. Normally I'd comment, but there's no time for that today.

"Hi," he says. "What's up?"

"We're looking for Murray," I say. "Is he here?"

"Hey, Rose." Murray appears beside Mark. He's dressed, at least, wearing plaid shorts and a Bob Marley T-shirt. He's holding his mandolin. "What's up? Oh, hey, Shilo. You guys want to do an early jam? I love it." Murray has a wide grin. It's hard not to smile back. But I'm on a mission.

"I'd love to jam—"

"My fiddle has a giant crack in it," I say, cutting off Shilo. "I heard your mom plays violin in the orchestra. Can you help?" No time for long explanations.

Murray frowns. "Hmm. I mean, I can try, but I don't really know much other than I heard there are a few good luthiers around."

Why didn't I think of this yesterday? With all the fiddlers here, there's got to be a few repair experts at the festival.

"But you know what?" Murray adds. "You know that guy Liam?"

"Um, yeah," I say.

"He definitely knows one of the luthiers. Yesterday he was telling me how she's from his town and how she travels from festival to festival.

I heard she's really good, like practically a magician, you know with glue and stuff. Why don't you ask him about her?"

"Do you know where he might be?" Magic is exactly what I need. "I have to talk to him right away. I have to get my fiddle fixed right away." My words cartwheel out.

"Okay, then, let's go." Murray grabs his mandolin case and shuts the door behind him.

The three of us wind our way back through the yurt maze. "Wait," I say. "Where exactly are we going?" It looks like we're leaving the performers' area. "Where is Liam? What's your plan?"

"It's all good," Murray says. "Try to relax. I know exactly where his stuff is. He's set up in the spectator area because he's basically crashing the festival."

We reach the edge of the tent city, the one we saw from the bus. All I can see are hundreds of tents, a sea of bright colors, all practically on top of each other. This will take forever.

"Come on," Murray says. Shilo and I follow.

We step between tents, the tent nylon brushing against my bare legs. Some doors have been tied open and I want to look inside, but I don't want to seem like a snoop. I see bare feet poking out of one tent, a few piles of dirty clothes, an empty guitar case.

We pass a cozy circle in the middle of a group of tents. I see campstoves perched on coolers, beat-up plastic bins and colorful blankets. A few girls older than me, wearing bandannas and long skirts, sit on the ground, drinking out of steel camping mugs, huge sunglasses partially covering their faces. They look so confident, so sure they are where they're supposed to be. I try to look casual, like I know exactly where I'm going.

"See over there?" Murray points toward what looks like a huge spiderweb nestled in the trees beside the tents. "That's the sticky tape web. Anyone can add to it." As we walk by, a few people unroll white tape and wind it around the already huge web. In the middle of the web some guys are sleeping, knit caps and sunglasses on.

"Whoa!" says Shilo. "This is crazy. And so fun-looking. I wish we could stay here."

I'm thinking the same thing. But I also like my privacy. Here, it looks like you couldn't sneeze in your tent without everyone knowing.

"It does smell a bit though," I say. Even in the fresh air on this sunny day, I catch a whiff of stinky feet.

"Wait until we pass the outhouses," Murray says with a grin. "You don't need a map to find them, just your nose. They are already starting to overflow."

"Okay, okay, we get it," I say, but I can't help smiling. "Where's Liam's tent? And how can you possibly find it?"

"All the tents kind of look the same," Shilo says. "It's like we're lost in a never-ending smelly tent world."

"Well, Liam doesn't have a tent," Murray says. "He has a little different setup."

I'm curious. How does Murray know so much about Liam when I'm the one who hung out with him for practically a whole day?

"Wait until you see it. It's kind of awesome," Murray says, laughing. "That way," he adds, moving toward yet another cluster of tents. This one is centered around a small wooden cart like the ones that might sell popcorn at a fair. "I remember this food stand. He's near here."

I look around and spot what looks like a giant lime-green sock with a zipper.

"That's Liam's," Murray says, walking straight up to the sock. "Cool, eh? Kind of a cross between a sleeping bag and a mini tent." He peers in through the mesh window "Looks like he's not home."

"Not exactly a surprise," I say. "It's tiny. I'd go nuts staying in there for long." I feel a strange mix of relief and disappointment that Liam is not here.

"I think it's kind of cute," says Shilo, walking over to peek through the mesh. "Like his own mini world."

"Hey, what's up?"

I whirl around and there's Liam, a thermos mug in one hand, a granola bar in the other. "I waved at you guys from the lineup, but you didn't see me. Didn't want to lose my place in the line."

"I love your mini tent," Shilo says.

"Thanks—"

"My fiddle got dropped the other night and there's a huge crack in it," I say, unzipping my case and gently pulling out my fiddle. I can barely stand to look at it.

"Man, that sucks," Liam says, reaching out to run his fingers along the crack.

"Murray says you know a luthier here. A good one," I say.

"Oh yeah, Grace. She's awesome. I've known her for years. I spent part of yesterday helping her out."

"Can she fix my fiddle? Like, right now?" I ask. What if I have to play on the spare fiddle? How can I possibly do my best on that thing?

"Sure, why not?" Liam says without hesitation. "I've got my breakfast. Let's go."

Sixteen

The four of us walk to Grace's tent without talking, dodging festivalgoers like we're in a video game. I am thinking about how long glue takes to dry.

"I'll wait outside." Shilo plunks down on some grass near the tent, then pulls her flute from its case. "I will entertain myself and others."

"I'll stay too," Murray says. Shilo looks like she just won a prize.

The luthier's tent is filled with fiddles, hanging on hooks from the ceiling and the walls. I reach up and gently touch a beautiful dark fiddle. Its striped pattern reminds me of flames. I rock the fiddle gently from side to side, allowing the sun to catch the fiery lines. The earthy smell of wood mingles with a slight chalky taste in the air from all the rosin. I could bottle all my years of playing into that smell, like a perfume.

"Liam?" A woman's voice pulls me into the moment. "You're back?" A woman with long gray hair and a friendly face greets us. "I could use all the help I can get. Most kids seem to want to volunteer for something near the Main Stage or backstage with the performers."

"Hi, Grace," Liam says with a smile. "This is my friend Rose."

"Hi," I say.

"Hello, Rose, welcome to my...workshop!" Grace says with a laugh.

"It was fun hanging out here yesterday. And maybe we can both help out for a bit today," Liam says. "But I was also wondering if we could show you Rose's fiddle. It's got a bit of an issue."

A bit of an issue? It's like an earthquake rocked through it. I feel my neck tense. Will this work?

"Of course," Grace says. "I'm working on a rush restoration right now and could really use some extra hands. Liam, maybe you can deal with any customers that come by looking for strings or things like that. Here's the cash box."

She hands him a plain metal box. "Prices are marked. Rose, why don't you come on over here with your fiddle?"

"Okay," I say. Grace seems familiar in some way, and I feel drawn to her.

She sits down at a long wooden table covered with strange-looking tools of all shapes and sizes, a mason jar of paintbrushes, and pieces of wood stacked at one end. Two bright lamps shine their light on a fiddle in the center. It looks destroyed. My face must show my shock.

"Looks worse than it is," Grace says with a small laugh. "But have no fear. I can get this fiddle back to making beautiful sounds."

She adjusts her beat-up wooden stool and leans forward over the fiddle, which is in two completely separate pieces.

"What happened to it?" The smell of fresh wood shavings draws me forward to take a closer look. I catch a whiff of something chemical but not overpowering.

"Here." Grace pats the stool next to her. "This is a performer's fiddle. It bounced out of the case and down onto the pavement when it was being unloaded from their band van."

"Ouch," I say, leaning forward to check out the damage.

"So I had to remove the top to glue a crack in the body." She reaches for a long, thin knife, which she dips into what looks like an ancient, dirty coffeemaker. Grace sees my expression and laughs.

"A little stinky, isn't it? Don't worry—I don't make coffee in this pot anymore. This is where I mix my glue." She pulls the knife out quickly and leans over the fiddle. She carefully edges the glue into the crack. I feel my neck start to relax.

"Kind of mesmerizing to watch, isn't it?" Grace glances up and smiles. She doesn't seem hurried.

"Yeah," I say, returning her smile. "Can you do this with any fiddle? Take it apart and put it back together again?"

"I can if there's a crack or a problem with the sound post." She puts down her knife carefully, cleaning the gluey edge off on a piece of scrap wood, and rubs her eyes with her arm.

I have to know if there's a chance. "My fiddle. It's broken," I blurt out. "And it's very special to me." For some reason I feel safe here. Like I've been here for days. And I don't want to leave.

Grace reaches over and places a hand on my arm, squeezing gently. "Yes, I'm sure it is special. Gives you strength even." I just nod, not wanting to sob. "Do you want to tell me more about it?"

Again the words tumble out. "It was my dad's. And I need it...my mom's coming. The final round...tomorrow..." I'm not making any sense.

"Okay, okay," she says gently. "Well, why don't we have a look?" She clears a spot and I scramble to my case, take out my fiddle and lay it down on the table. Grace takes a look, gently moving her fingers along the crack.

"This is fixable. But I'll need to take the back off, fix the crack and then glue it back on."

"How long will that take?" I ask, calculating the hours left until the contest.

"I'm not sure it will be dry by tomorrow," Grace says. "No promises, but I'll try."

I nod and sag down on the stool. She gets to work, using a long sharp tool to carefully release the back.

"There, I've almost got the back off. Then we'll be able to see the whole inside and assess the damage properly."

I hold my breath. She carefully pulls off the back and then flips it over. Inside, I can see a carefully painted flower. A white rose with soft, open petals, trailed by a black, curved stem studded with thorns.

"Did you know about this?" Grace asks. I shake my head.

Liam has wandered over to the table and looks with interest at the painting. "Cool," he says.

"It's much more than just cool," says Grace, looking right at me. "Instruments are not just for music. They can be art. Carvings, pictures, words—they all bring a little bit more magic to an instrument. Your fiddle and this painting are very special. It would be interesting to find out who the artist was." She picks her knife up again and reaches for the glue.

"Do you think your dad knew?" Liam asks.

"I have no idea," I say. A white rose. If only I could ask him.

Seventeen

"I hope that everyone had a good day." Ms. O'Krancy smiles from the head of our dinner table. The whole fiddle group has gathered. After we were done at Grace's tent, Shilo, Murray, Liam and I went to the last half of the Celtic String Band workshop.

The meal tent is jammed with performers, everyone talking about the final contest round tomorrow. All I can think about is the white rose inside my fiddle. Whether my dad knew it was there. And if the glue will be dry by morning.

"Why aren't we allowed to have our cell phones?" Emilia asks. "I really want to listen to some recordings." I tune out as Ms. O'Krancy starts explaining how it's good to "unplug" once in a while.

"I need to prove to my mom I'm taking music seriously," I say in a whisper to Shilo. "Otherwise she's going to cancel my lessons. Especially now that I've broken my dad's fiddle."

"I don't get it," Shilo says, shaking her head. "You *are* serious about music. Why can't she see that?"

I sigh. "I wish I knew."

"Look, there's Robin Ross," Shilo says. "I think she's sitting with some of the musicians from Lunar." We watch as Robin says something and the table breaks out in laughter. "I am dying to go ask her for an autograph," Shilo adds. "But don't worry—I won't."

"The other day she told me about some college called Berklee. I want to know more about it." I imagine myself onstage with Robin Ross. I would improvise an amazing harmony part, and then she would introduce me as the young fiddler to watch. I shake off the daydream. First I need to win the contest.

"You have to go talk to her," Shilo says. I want to, but I don't have the nerve.

"Any more questions?" Ms. O'Krancy's voice pulls my attention back to our table. "You all did a great job at our performance. Those of you in the fiddle-contest final are ready. We'll all be there to cheer you on. Make sure you get to bed early tonight!" She picks up her plate and, as if on cue, everyone starts talking all at once. I look over at Robin's table again.

"Go." Shilo nudges me, but I can see she is only half focused on me. Murray is sitting across the table from us but has turned to watch tonight's performance. After every meal one of the performing groups jams together. Tonight it's a guy on a ukulele and a woman on a cello. I stop obsessing for a few minutes to listen. But something inside tells me this is my chance.

"I'm going over there," I say, standing up from the bench and grabbing my plate. Robin was so friendly before. Why shouldn't I go talk to her? I'm a performer too.

I weave through the tables. The music makes it difficult to walk slowly, because the duo is playing an upbeat jig, and the cellist is doing some crazy percussive sounds on her instrument. I reach Robin's table in what feels like one breath. But just as I take the last step, the whole table erupts in laughter again. I veer left and keep my eyes looking ahead of me, like I'm looking for someone across the room.

When I reach the bussing station with my plate, I'm deflated like a wrinkly used balloon. I dump my plate and slowly scan the room, playing it cool. Robin is still at her table. I can't do it. But I don't want to go back to our table either, so I head out the nearest entrance and flop down at a picnic table covered in gross dishes that lazy people did not clear.

If I can't talk to Robin, then I should go and practice my tunes. But I'm worried about seeing my mom tomorrow. What if she takes away my dad's fiddle and my lessons?

Music is all I've ever wanted to do. But maybe it's time to get real. Maybe I should start picturing myself as a soloist in front of an orchestra, wearing a beautiful gown and playing the classics.

I remember the day my dad took me to my first violin lesson. My mom was in law school at the time, and my dad worked at night, so he was always the one to take me places.

We pulled up to an old house on the east side of town. My dad knocked on a battered door that looked too small for him to fit through. He smiled down at me and squeezed my free hand. My other hand clutched the violin-case handle. A tiny woman with dark hair answered the door. Her name was Karen, and she had won a place in the city orchestra when she was only nineteen. She trained me well in the classics. But she also taught me a lot about the Celtic music I love so much. She grew up on the east coast of Canada, playing past her bedtime with her parents at kitchen parties. Maybe somehow I could play both kinds of music too.

My vision of myself in a fancy dress, playing Bach in the orchestra, keeps getting shoved aside by one of the new tunes I just learned in the string workshop. The Scottish reel makes me picture a lot of stomping black boots. I want to be part of that kind of frenetic, delirious energy.

Just then Robin bursts out of the meal tent. I scramble to catch up to her. People stroll in every direction, and I have to keep my gaze on the case on her back, which bobs up and down as she walks.

The case stops. A woman coming from the other direction has stopped Robin. I scurry forward. The other person gives Robin a hug and then continues on. Now's my chance.

"Robin!" I call out. "I was wondering if I could ask you a couple more—"

"I'm so sorry," she interrupts, "but I've got to get ready for my performance in fifteen minutes." She smiles. "But find me later, okay?"

I stand there feeling like a complete idiot. People keep streaming by. I'm blocking the path. Robin was kind and what she said made sense, but I still feel like I did in third grade when I was the only girl not invited to Emilia's birthday party.

I'm dreading seeing my mom tomorrow more than ever. Some way, somehow, I have to make her understand.

Eighteen

When I wake up the next morning, the first thing I see is the spare fiddle.

I sit up like I was stung by a wasp.

"Good morning, sleepyhead," Shilo says. She's standing in front of the tiny mirror, putting on lip gloss.

"I gotta go check out my fiddle," I say.

"What about breakfast?"

"I'm not hungry," I say, whipping on yesterday's clothes. "I'm going to run over and see about my fiddle. Right now." I shove my sneakers on and bang out the yurt door. The glue had all night to dry. It had to work. My mom is on her way.

I hurry through the Marketplace in the still-cool morning air. When I spot Grace's tent I break into a run.

I stop in front of the tent to catch my breath. Then I enter, carefully weaving through the fiddles hanging from the ceiling.

"Grace," I call out as I make my way toward the work table. "It's Rose."

She's not there. And I don't see my fiddle on the table. Does that mean it's fixed and she's trying to find me? Or that she couldn't fix it? I have a horrible urge to smash something. I turn around and almost run smack into Grace. She puts her arms up and gently takes my hands.

"Oh, sorry to frighten you," she says, her voice calm. "I knew I'd see you today, but it's pretty early."

"Oh, yeah, sorry," I say. But I need to know. "Um, where's my fiddle?"

She keeps a hold on my hands and squeezes them a bit.

"Well," she says. "I was able to take the back off and repair the crack—"

"Okay, good," I say. "So can I play it today?"

"But I had to wait for that glue to dry overnight," Grace continues, ignoring my interruption. "Today I'll glue the back piece on." She pauses. "But it will take all day to dry.

If you try to play your fiddle before the glue is completely dry, you could damage it further."

I stare down at our joined hands as her words sink in. I won't be able to play my dad's fiddle in the contest.

"Rose," Grace says. "Listen. I know this fiddle is special to you, but just play the other one like you always do. Bring your heart to your tunes."

I wrench my hands away and run out of the tent, biting my lip to keep from crying.

Outside, the sun blinds me and I feel disoriented. A smiling couple holding hands walks by me. I smell coffee and cinnamon as they pass. It triggers a memory of my dad bringing me a cinnamon bun in the morning, coffee in hand, foot tapping to music in his head. He was often out late at night, performing. But he still got up early to be with me. And he kept on going. Until he couldn't.

I think of what Grace said. And then of my dad's words. *No hesitation.*

I start to run. There are only a few hours left before the fiddle contest. I'm going to spend every minute practicing my tunes.

* * *

"Guess what?" Shilo squeals as I step into our yurt. "Murray asked me to work on a tune together when we get home, him on fiddle, me on Irish flute! Plus, I'm meeting him before the contest. He says he's nervous and wants company. What's up with your fiddle?"

"The glue's not dry," I say. "I'm playing the spare fiddle."

"Oh." She pauses. "Do you want to borrow mine?"

I hug her. "You're the best," I say. "Your fiddle has great sound. But I've never played it before. At least I've been playing the spare for the last few days. I'm getting used to it."

The contest starts right after lunch. Part of me would rather just curl up in bed right now. Not face my mom. But the contest is my chance.

I pick up the spare fiddle and check the strings. The last thing I want is another broken string. I play some scales to relax. Focusing on the slow vibrations calms me, even on the plywood fiddle. I run through my tunes. Shilo has gone off to meet Murray now, and I'm happy to be alone for a while. I don't want to face the nervous energy of the performers' meal tent, so I eat lunch from my stash of granola bars. I have to force myself to chew and swallow.

Finally it's time. I pack up the fiddle, take one last look in the mirror and head out to the Main Stage.

I hear the crowd before I see it. I step carefully over the gnarled roots along the well-worn dirt path, and as I reach the clearing I see what looks like a zillion more people than at the first round.

"Whoa." I can barely see any grass. There are blankets and beach chairs and kids running wild. People cluster in small groups, talking excitedly. Around the edges of the crowd, fiddlers frantically rehearse. I look up at the stage. It's empty but for a few microphones. My mouth feels dry from the granola bars, like I can't swallow. I take a swig of water.

"Rose!"

I hear my name and scan the crowd. It's Anna. Shilo is with her.

"I'll go see where you are in the order of play," Shilo offers and heads toward the stage.

"I want to rehearse one last time," I say to Anna. Thankfully, she leaves me alone at the edge of the crowd. Onstage, the festival organizer is at the microphone, saying something about the sponsors.

I spot Liam on the edge of the crowd. He's sitting on the grass by himself, holding his fiddle guitar style. He looks calm. I look away before he sees me. I have to concentrate. I pull the spare fiddle from its case. It's ugly. I play through my reel to warm up. My fingers tangle as I'm crossing strings, and for a moment I feel like someone has ripped the tunes from my memory.

"Rose." Shilo runs up. "You're up third. You need to go wait by the stage."

I feel dizzy. Shilo pulls me toward stage left, where we are supposed to wait. The first contestant is onstage playing "Westphalia Waltz," and I can tell by her shaking bow that she must be very nervous. Like me. My palms start to slick up with sweat, and I put my fiddle in my other hand.

"Hi again."

I look up, and there's Liam standing on the first stair leading up to the stage.

"It's pretty funny that we're playing one after the other."

"Hey. Well, at least I get to see you in action first," I stutter. He's shattering my focus.

"From this close, you'll be able to hear all my mistakes." He grins. I seriously doubt he will make any.

"I'm going to go find a good spot to watch you," Shilo says. "Good luck!" A quick hug and she's off. The girl onstage finishes to polite applause. She bows and exits the stage on the other side.

"I'm up," Liam says. "Wish me luck." The announcer calls his name. Liam jogs up the stairs, marches to the microphone and gives a nod toward the judges' table. I see his toe tapping out a beat already. He raises his bow and starts into a fast-paced reel. The crowd claps and stomps. For his second piece he plays an energetic waltz that gets a few people dancing up front.

He moves smoothly to his tune of choice, and my whole body freezes. It can't be. Not again. The same one I picked! "The Coulin," an Irish air, one I thought no one else would choose. I can't believe my bad luck.

Liam makes the haunting long notes both uplifting and wistful. The audience is silent.

Even though I'm furious, I shut my eyes and let the sounds wave through me. It's mesmerizing, and I know it's challenging to play smoothly. I have to admit, Liam plays it very well.

I need to choose something else. People will think I'm copying him if I play the same tune.

Liam wraps it up with a gentle vibrato, just as I would. The crowd erupts in applause. I grip my bow so hard, the edge digs into my palm. That was supposed to be my moment, my tune. A woman appears next to me, holding a clipboard.

"Be ready to walk onstage as soon as he starts walking off the far side," she says in my ear.

Liam bows and quickly exits. I stand there, motionless. The woman nudges me with her clipboard. I scamper up, almost tripping on the last stair. My ears feel plugged, like I'm underwater. I drag myself to the microphone. I manage to plaster on a smile, but my face feels like clay.

The crowd waits. I hear a familiar voice. "Go, Rose!" Shilo's cheer seems to unglue my body, and I raise my fiddle to my chin. I take a small step back to make sure I'm not too close to the microphone.

I tap my foot to count myself in and play. My reel choice is "Mason's Apron," which I've played for years and know inside out. It rolls off my fingers, my bow arm moving as though driven by puppet strings. An echo from the sound system bounces back to me, and my fiddle sounds too loud, too harsh. I take another small step back. I focus on my fingers darting on the fingerboard and add some ornaments to make the tune my own. The crowd is clapping, so I must be doing okay.

I move into the waltz. "Ashokan Farewell" is popular and will probably be played five times tonight. But I needed something really familiar since I don't have my fiddle. I focus on my vibrato and try to squeeze some good sound out of the plywood fiddle.

As I play the last notes of the waltz, a memory of my dad and a tune he taught me comes to mind. It was one of the first tunes I learned from him. He would play three notes and I would echo them back until I had learned the whole thing. It's a simple, beautiful melody, difficult because the entire tune is played on two strings at a time. To me, it reaches out to somewhere beyond, a place I can't describe.

It's perfect. I take a deep breath, count in and then dive right in. No hesitation. When I'm done, I'm not even sure whether I played all the repeats. I just bow and walk off the stage.

Nineteen

I find a place to sit in the audience. I don't want to talk to anyone, not even Shilo. The rest of the contestants blur together. Each performer seems to sound better than I ever could. But I feel strangely calm in my little bubble of strangers.

"Hi." I turn and find myself face-to-face with my mom. She looks out of place, even though she's wearing old jeans and a striped T-shirt, her working-in-the-garden weekend clothes. "I saw you play and watched you move down here after your set." Her eyes look a little shiny.

"Oh. Hi." I wish the ground would open up and swallow me. I brace myself for the lecture. I'm doomed.

"I thought you played very nicely. Especially the last tune," she says quietly. "I'm sorry you weren't able to play it on your dad's violin." I look away. She knows everything. Anna must have told her.

"Yeah, well, don't bother being nice to me. I know you're planning on taking my fiddle away and canceling my lessons," I say. She doesn't reply. I can't stop the words. "How can you possibly say I'm not serious about music?"

I'm nearly shouting now, but the performer onstage has everyone stomping their feet to a reel, so it doesn't matter.

"Maybe I should go live with Shilo and Anna. At least there I would be able to play the music I want. And you wouldn't have to deal with me. You could forget about me. About Dad." I'm crying now and not even sure what I'm saying. But instead of putting on her lecture face, Mom puts her arms around me. She hugs me. Tight. I let her. I feel all the worries from the week pouring out of me in tears.

"I don't want you to go," she whispers. "You're the only one I have left. I know you miss him so much. So do I, even though that's really hard for me to admit. And I'm sorry. I was wrong to say you weren't serious about music. I was just scared for you. The life of a musician is not an easy one. Your dad worked so hard and sacrificed so much just to make ends meet. But when I saw you up there onstage, I could see that you love it. Just like he did. Even when you're unhappy, performing comes naturally to you. Maybe you don't even know that. I started thinking about all the hours of practice you've put in, for so many years. No one ever made you do that. It was all you. Your choice."

Maybe I'm not doomed. "Wow. Thanks, Mom. Yeah, I've been angry with myself for not knowing all the tunes. I feel like I could have worked so much harder, should be better at learning the tunes by ear, better at improvising." It feels so good to let all my worries out. "And I'm so mad at myself for wrecking Dad's fiddle," I say, sniffing. "But it's being repaired by an expert right now."

Mom squeezes my shoulders. "Yes, and that is probably going to cost quite a bit. Good thing I'm here, right?"

Okay, so at least I know my mom hasn't been replaced by a super-nice robot version. I shrug. I hadn't actually considered how I was going to pay Grace. I was completely caught up in just getting the fiddle fixed. I guess moms *are* good to have around sometimes.

"Ladies and gentlemen!" The announcer interrupts us on a scratchy mic. "The Grand Prize winner will be announced in five minutes." At least it will be over soon and I can slink away.

"We should move closer to the stage," Mom says, squeezing my hand. "You should be ready."

"What for?" I say. "There's no way I'll win. I changed tunes at the last minute. I should have chosen a waltz with more energy. I totally didn't feel it."

"Let's go." She pulls me along. We step around blankets covered in water bottles and snacks—even past one with a sleeping baby. We find Shilo and Anna.

Now that I'm this close, I start wondering if I actually have a chance. My heart bangs so loudly I'm afraid I'll pass out. What if they choose Liam and me as co-winners? Would we both get to go onstage with Lunar?

The announcer calls the second- and third-place winners. Not me. Not Liam. There's still a chance.

"And now, the moment you've all been waiting for," the announcer says. "Make sure you come out tonight to hear this fiddler perform live onstage with Lunar." He pauses.

"It was a close call. All the performers were magnificent. They are the future of our industry!" He pauses again. *Just get on with it!*

"The Grand Prize winner is Murray Cummings!"

Murray? Shilo and I look at each other in shock. I swing around and see Ms. O'Krancy and Murray heading toward the stage. Murray has a huge smile on his face, but he looks stunned.

"Way to go, Murray!" Shilo screams. Anna and Mom are clapping wildly. I start to clap too, stiffly at first, but soon I'm cheering right alongside Shilo.

"He was amazing," Shilo says. She's right, I realize. I heard him play, but I was so wrapped up in my own stuff that I wasn't truly listening.

After a long hug from Ms. O'Krancy, Murray makes his way onto the stage. One of the fiddlers from Lunar is there too. She shakes Murray's hand. I see Liam across the crowd. He is jumping up and down and clapping for Murray. I wonder how he feels inside. I think of my own performance. Only the last tune I played came from my heart. But that one tune did feel good.

"There's always next year," Mom says. "Now how about we go and see how your violin is doing? After that we can talk about how you broke curfew."

Twenty

"**H**ey there." As Mom and I inch away from the Main Stage, I hear a voice. I whirl around and see Robin Ross. "Did ya'll enjoy yourselves? I saw you up there earlier and remembered you wanted to talk to me. Did you want to hear more about Berklee College?"

"Um, yeah," I say, stumbling over my words. Mom stands next to me, a curious expression on her face. "I was really interested in what you told me about that school. I'm taking classical lessons right now"—I steal a glance at my mom—"but I want to learn about all kinds of music."

"Well, Berklee is the place for that. I bet you would fit right in. You sounded great up there. You're a natural."

"Really?" I want to believe her, but I didn't even place. "I had to change my tune of choice at the very last minute because the performer who went onstage right before me played the same one."

Robin nods and laughs. "Yep, that's happened to me before. That's how you learn to roll with the punches, you know? And you came up with another tune that sounded great. That's what being a musician is all about." Robin waves at someone ahead of us in the crowd. "Well, I have to get rolling now, but yeah, you check out Berklee's website. It's a great place to study if you're serious about being a musician. Good luck!"

As she disappears into the crowd, I can't stop smiling. She said I was a natural!

"Mom?" I say, turning to her. "When we get home, can you tell me more about when you and Dad used to play together? I found a picture in Dad's fiddle case. You were playing the flute in the picture. You looked so happy."

My mom's eyes fill with tears. For a second I feel mad again. She still won't talk to me. But she hugs me for the second time today, then lets go and smiles.

"Those times with your dad were some of the happiest of my life," she says. "But I stopped playing when I went to law school and never seemed to find the time to pick it up again. I felt like I had lost all my ability. I was embarrassed to even try." She squeezes my hand. "But yes, when we get home we will talk. And I want to hear more about Berklee too. After seeing you up on the stage today, I'm thinking that it just might be the perfect place for you to study music. Maybe you could start with a summer program."

What is happening? As we weave through the crowd I'm amazed by how confidently my mom moves. Like maybe she's been to festivals before. In another time. I have so many questions.

"Which way?" Mom asks. I grab her hand, and now it's me leading her through the crowd. We reach Grace's tent and enter, heading straight to the back. At the workbench, huddled over a guitar in pieces, sit Grace and Liam. He looks up and smiles. I grin back like an idiot.

"Good news." Grace smiles. "Your fiddle came together nicely. You can see where the crack was, but I believe the sound has been restored. I hope you don't mind, but I asked Liam to play a tune for me so I could test it. He plays so well and I wanted to hear what your lovely fiddle could do." She reaches behind her and takes my fiddle down from a violin stand.

"I don't mind at all," I say, reaching out to take the fiddle. I hold it in my hands, savoring the warm wood once again. I turn it over. I can barely see the crack line. "Wow, thanks so much!"

"It was my pleasure," Grace replies. "Did you find out who painted the rose?"

"Oh, that was me," my mom says, extending her hand. "I'm Claire, Rose's mom. The fiddle, and the painting inside, was a gift from me to my husband."

"*You* did that?" I sputter. "You paint?"

My mom smiles a real smile. Just like the one in the picture with my dad from long ago. "Yeah, believe it or not, I even went to art school," she says with a wink. "I can show you some of my work when we get home."

I stare, wondering what other surprises she's going to spring on me. This has been one weird day.

"Go ahead," Grace says to me. "See how it sounds. Take it outside if you like."

Liam nods toward the back door of the tent, his fiddle under his arm. My mom and Grace are talking, so I head out with Liam, my dad's fiddle placed carefully under my arm.

"I think it's pretty cool that Murray won," Liam says. "He played awesome. I thought I might at least place, but hey, I guess you never know what the judges will like. I'm definitely going to watch him tonight with Lunar."

"Me too," I say. "Sorry I missed your People's Choice performance. I bet you were awesome."

He smiles. "I was scared, but I think I pulled off at least a few tunes the way I wanted to."

"Nice. So are you coming back next year?" I try to memorize everything about him. His dark hair. His fiddle. The hands that move with grace. And the hat, always the hat. When I'm back home I want to remember him just like this. Right in this moment.

"I don't know. I'm still going to look into that whole farm-intern thing. Who knows where that will lead. You?"

"I'm definitely coming back," I say. "Hey, I know I got all caught up with my broken fiddle and everything, but thanks a lot for bringing me to the session the other night."

Liam smiles. "Yeah, that was pretty cool. I love that you can show up in a room and learn music you've never heard with people you've mostly never met."

"But didn't you know most of the tunes?" I ask.

"I knew some," he says. "But I did a lot of faking. Didn't you?"

I smile a huge smile. "Yep, sometimes." So I'm not the only one! I need to remember this in the future. "Okay, let's play."

"You pick the tune," Liam says. "I'll play harmony."

"'Skye Boat,'" I say, smiling. "Simple and classic, remember?" Liam nods and brings his fiddle up under his chin. Our eyes meet, and we start on the same breath.

We may not be onstage together, like the picture on the festival website, but we're playing together right now. I know my mom will still punish me somehow for breaking curfew. But she's promised to tell me stories about my dad and her art. And she's willing to talk about Berklee! She will probably still nag me as much as ever, but I think it will be different between us from now on.

As I travel through the melody, the music erases all the chatter in my head. In this moment, I'm good.

Acknowledgments

The music festival in this book is fictional, a strange and wonderful combination of the many festivals and workshops I have attended over the past decade.

Thanks to Dave and Owen for everything. Thanks to my critique partner, Kim Woolcock, for being the best writing "co-worker." Thank you to my editor at Orca, Tanya Trafford. Thanks to her encouragement and her editorial super-powers, this story was infinitely improved. And a shout-out to all the musicians I have played with and learned from over the years—thanks for the music, thanks for the inspiration!

MEGAN CLENDENAN is a freelance writer and editor. When she's not writing, she spends her time running or biking through her local mountains or trying to play her violin. She lives in North Vancouver, British Columbia, with her family and their two incredibly fuzzy orange cats. *Offbeat* is her first novel. For more information, visit meganclendenan.com.